7

JUNIOR CLASSICS

Published by
Rupa Publications India Pvt. Ltd 2016
7/16, Ansari Road, Daryaganj
New Delhi 110002

Sales centres:
Bengaluru Chennai
Hyderabad Jaipur Kathmandu
Kolkata Mumbai Prayagraj

This is a work of fiction. Names, characters, places and incidents are either the product of the author's imagination or are used fictitiously and any resemblance to any actual person, living or dead, events or locales is entirely coincidental.

P-ISBN: 978-81-291-3891-0
E-ISBN: 978-81-291-4330-3

Third impression 2023

10 9 8 7 6 5 4 3

Printed in India

Contents

The Last of the Mohicans

James Fenimore Cooper

It was 1757, in the area around New York between the Hudson River and Lake George, France and England were fighting for colonial dominance in the region. The battle was less furious compared to the toils and dangers of the wilderness. The swiftly flowing streams and rugged mountains were ample proofs of the nature's hostility in the area that stretched from the frontiers of Canada. Nevertheless, the Europeans were seeking newer ways to spread their power far and wide.

With a huge army, Marquis de Montcalm, the French general, was marching towards Fort William Henry, one of the English stronghold areas. They were seemingly in a position of advantage and control because some of the natives were guiding them in the unfamiliar territory.

Still, the Englishmen were somehow on a firm ground across several forts. It was evident from the information they would get to help in their preparation for any possible event.

Magua, a native informer, brought the news about the advancing Frenchmen. At Ford Edward commanded by General Webb, Magua arrived with the message that Commander Munro needed more men at Fort William Henry.

Webb planned to send the reinforcements that included 1,500 men. First he could only instruct Major Duncan Heyward to go with Munro's daughters, Alice and Cora to see their father. And Magua was leading and guiding them back to Fort William Henry across the rough terrains of the mountain.

'Is such a ghostly figure always present in the woods, or is this a special entertainment ordered on our behalf?' Alice asked.

Alice was disrespectfully referring to Magua when she asked Heyward.

'The Indian is a "runner" for the army. He has volunteered to guide us to the fort through a shortcut that none of us know,' replied the major.

However her elder sister, Cora was a kinder soul, and she had no issue with any people even if they looked different.

On the way, the travellers came across a man, who claimed that his name was David Gamut and that he was a psalmody-singer. He started singing psalms and hymns. Upon asking, he replied he wanted to accompany them to the fort. Heyward was unwilling but Alice insisted to allow him join the band. She argued that the man could be a disciple of Apollo, the Greek god of poetry and music.

In another corner of the mountain—an hour away from Heyward and his company—two men were walking by a rapid stream. The first man,

Hawkeye, was a white hunter with a rifle and a knife. He was accompanied by a Mohican named Chingachgook, who was carrying a tomahawk and an English-made knife.

As they passed by the stream, they talked about the plight of the natives. They talked about the truth in the Bible and the techniques of fighting. They also talked about the Mohicans and their forefathers; besides how their entire race had disappeared. Only Chingachgook and his son, Uncas, were the last of the Mohicans.

Incidentally, Uncas appeared and informed the two older men how he had been following the enemies, the Maquas who were also known as the Mengwe or the Iroquois. Before long they heard the sound of the Englishmen and their horses.

'Who are you, riding among the beasts and dangers in this wilderness?' Hawkeye asked Major Heyward.

'We are the believers in religion and friends to the law and to the king,' replied Heyward.

'You are, then, lost,' interrupted the hunter. 'It seems you don't know which is the right or the left.'

'We have lost our guide. We are heading to Fort William Henry. Do you know which way is it?'

Hawkeye was initially surprised. And it was almost shocking when he learnt that a native was guiding them. It was impossible for an Indian to lose his way in the wood that was his second home.

The suspicion was confirmed when it was learnt that the guide was a Maqua, who was derisively called a Mingo. Hawkeye explained how a Mingo was believed to be dishonest. They made a plan to capture the guide, who rejoined them shortly, while the hunters hid in a thicket.

Magua was astonished when a sound came from the bush. Immediately he fled while the others gave him a chase.

Some of them wanted to pursue further but the dusk was approaching. The night meant more danger so they gave up. Instead they made a new plan to proceed.

Their horses were an issue. On one hand, they could not afford to make any noise that could compromise their safety and life. The rider-less horses, on the other hand, could mislead their enemies. So they hid the horses while on a canoe they navigated upstream toward Glenn's Fall on the Hudson. They were going to take shelter in a cave, just beside the waterfall.

All the others had apparently slept but Hawkeye and the Mohicans were standing guard in the shadow of the night.

Soon it became clear that Magua had intentionally misled them earlier in the day. Just before the daybreak, the Iroquois men arrived and started attacking.

Gamut was taken aback in the first few rounds of gunfires and was wounded with a shot. Heyward took the two sisters to the outer cave, where Cora reminded him how much the major was important for their safety and journey.

The two parties were taking guard when Hawkeye saw four enemies swimming in the swift stream. They shot down two of them. Five more Iroquois were killed when the battle was getting closer, as they started fighting hand to hand. This was clearly the Indian way of fighting, as Heyward learnt the hard way. He was dragged down but fortunately Uncas came to his rescue.

Cora turned to Uncas and told him, 'Go to my father, and tell him to speed up the rescue process and ask him to look forward with confidence to meet his children again.'

The idea was also reasonable because the Indian would not hurt the women. Though Uncas was reluctant to leave Cora, he trod towards the river. Chingachgook and Hawkeye followed him.

Only Heyward stayed back.

He said, 'There are evils worse than death. My presence can help avoid any such misfortune.'

Very soon, the ambience changed completely. The quiet, natural sound of the surrounding had engulfed the loud noises of the fighting completely. And there were four of them: Heyward, Cora, Alice and Gamut, who were inside the cave.

Then they heard a burst of voices, 'La Longue Carabine!'

It meant a Long Rifle in French. The Indians were calling for the white hunter.

'La Longue Carabine! La Longue Carabine!'

The place echoed with the yelling. Heyward remembered it was the name of a famous hunter and scout of the English camp. He also learnt it was a nickname of Hawkeye. Their only hope was to elude the search party.

The Indians were clearly disappointed to see the casualties from their side but none from the enemies. But they were helpless.

After a brief scuffle, the four of them were led out of the cave. Outside, there was a group of Hurons rejoicing the capture and they surrounded the frightened captives.

Heyward asked Magua to translate the things the natives were talking about. The latter spoke:

'The Hurons are asking for the hunter who knows the paths through the woods. La Longue Carabine! His rifle is good, and his eye never shut. And you should tell us where he is.'

'He is gone—escaped; he is far beyond their reach,' the major replied.

'He is not dead, but escaped. But why did you stay back?'

'The white man thinks none but cowards desert their women.'

Heyward got the upper hand of the argument. He talked to Magua to win his favour but in vain. Instead the Indian asked for Cora, though the major was reluctant. Magua told the lady how he wished to take revenge on Commander Munro. The commander had whipped him for misconduct a few years ago. He wanted to avenge this by marrying Cora, though she declined right away. Magua became furious and ask his men to torture the prisoners.

With his tomahawk, he chopped off a lock of Alice's hair and this compelled Heyward to thrash an Indian. Another Indian assaulted the major, but he was saved by an unknown gunshot that killed his attacker on the spot.

Everybody was whispering the name of 'La Longue Carabine' and this was followed by a wild and a sort of plaintive howl.

Hawkeye and the Mohicans had been hiding in a bush while piling up their arms. After the first deadly shot, they appeared and rushed towards the Hurons, waving their weapons.

Another round of hand-to-hand fighting started between the two groups. When one of the natives tried to hit Cora, Uncas struck the man and on the other side, Chingachgook was wrestling with Magua. In a while, Magua escaped after faking he was dead; and he disappeared among the bushes. And soon the fight was over as the remaining Hurons had fled for their lives.

Before leaving the place, the four released prisoners, along with the hunters, prepared and had their dinner. Then Hawkeye suggested the group should leave.

It was in the late afternoon when they began their journey again. The setting sun was enough to guide their way and the colour of the lively forest, in green, was slowly changing into a darker shade. Shortly they came across a blockhouse, which was as well a memorial site.

Chingachgook narrated how they had fought a fateful battle in that area many years ago. Then Hawkeye added how the Indian and his son were the last of the Mohicans.

At nightfall, Major Heyward volunteered for guarding the place, but Hawkeye refused.

'The eyes of a white man are too heavy and too blind for such a watch as this! The Mohican will be our sentinel, therefore let us sleep,' the hunter told the major.

The group were awakened at daybreak when they heard a sound. It was a group of Hurons who had lost their way. When one of them saw the blockhouse, he reacted with surprise. But all of them went away without even trying to enter.

It was Hawkeye again who knew the story.

He spoke, 'Ay! They respect the dead, and it has this time saved their own lives, and, it may be, the lives of better men too.'

Then without delaying, they resumed the journey towards the fort. They arrived near Fort William Henry, which the French, under General Montcalm, had besieged from the outside recently. As they went closer, they saw a French sentinel with whom Heyward started a conversation to distract him. Cora also joined the conversation while convincing the sentinel that they were members of the French army.

Meanwhile Chingachgook crept up and killed the sentinel. Suddenly, firing broke out between the French and the English armies, which this posed a threat to the travellers. However, the thick fog of the mountains rescued them. The battle was in full swing when they arrived at the fort out of harm's way.

They saw Colonel Munro when they entered the fort.

'Father! Father!' said Alice.

The colonel was overjoyed.

'For this I thank thee, Lord! Let danger come as it will, thy servant is now prepared!'

After their arrival, five days had passed amidst gunfight and occasional breaks. Munro had a huge task as it turned out that General Webb at Ford Edward had delayed sending more armies. Ironically, it was Magua who had brought the news about the required reinforcements.

'You have anticipated my wishes, Major Heyward,' Colonel Munro told Major Heyward one afternoon.

'I am sorry to see, sir. The messenger has returned in custody of the French! I hope there is no reason to distrust his loyalty?'

Apparently the French had captured Hawkeye.

'The fidelity of "The Long Rifle" is well known to me,' replied Munro, 'He is above suspicion; though his usual good fortune seems, at last, to have failed.'

Fortunately, the French released Hawkeye though General Montcalm kept back the letter that Webb had sent. In fact, the general also asked for an appointment with Munro, who in turn asked Major Heyward to go instead.

When he went to meet the general, Heyward saw Magua at the French camp. The Indian smiled wickedly but Heyward ignored it.

Later the general told him there were nearly 20,000 French soldiers, compared to 8,000 on the English side.

General Montcalm repeated the number, 'Some six or eight thousand men, whom their leader wisely judges to be safer in their works than in the field.'

He was implying that the Englishmen should surrender to them.

When Heyward came back and went to inform Munro, the colonel was with his daughters. The colonel was least interested in the French's threat to surrender. Instead he blamed

Heyward of being prejudiced, for preferring Alice to Cora. As a matter of fact, Cora had darker skin.

The colonel explained that Cora was his daughter from his first wife, who was from the West Indies. Alice was born after the death of the first wife, when he married his childhood friend in Scotland.

Later in the day, the colonel and the major set out for the French cantonment.

General Montcalm greeted them, saying to Munro, 'I am rejoiced, monsieur, that you have given us the pleasure of your company on this occasion.'

Munro was astonished when he was handed the letter. General Webb had asked them to surrender for they could not send any help.

The general further insisted to the Englishmen that surrendering would serve them the best. This would allow the English garrison to retain their arms, the colours and their baggage, and consequently—according to military opinion—their honour. Besides, the French assured them that the Indians would not attack them.

Munro accepted the offer though he was dejected. He left Heyward to complete the arrangement. The Englishmen were leaving the next morning.

It was August in 1757. The English were leaving the fort, as the whole valley was echoing with the drum signal of the surrender ceremony. The horns of the victors sounded long and merry while the British fifes blew a shrill tone until they became mute. Slowly, in columns, the English got out of the fort.

Soon, an Indian grabbed the shawl of a woman who protested impulsively. The minor incident soon became a disaster, when the Indian snatched and killed her baby. The mother was then with a tomahawk. It was horrible beyond expression.

Magua gave a signal by whooping. More than 2,000 Indians emerged from the woods and turned the place into a killing field. Everybody was running from one corner to another while the Hurons let loose a savage attack.

Alice was calling for her father while Gamut belted out a devotional song. Magua was delighted to see his prisoners. In such an instant, the Indian proposed Cora for marriage and as always, she refused. Then Magua grabbed

Alice and hopped on a horse, signalling Cora to do the same on another horse. The elder sister consented, for it was a necessity. Gamut saw it and he followed as well. As they rode, they came across the area where the Hurons were looting the victims and the sound slowly fades out.

Three days had passed after the killing outside the fort. The area still smelled of death and violence. At dusk, the five men—Hawkeye, Chingachgook, Uncas, Munro and Heyward—arrived to take stock of the situation. Munro broke down thinking about his daughter, when the younger Mohican found Cora's green riding-veil.

'Huh!' said Uncas.

'What is it, boy?' asked Hawkeye.

'My child!' Munro could not hide his emotion, 'Give me my child!'

They also found Gamut's horn. So there was a hope that the captives might be still alive. Heyward wanted to pursue immediately, but Hawkeye reasoned it was better to plan than to rush thoughtlessly. They made a plan for the next day and dozed off after having dinner.

Before daybreak, they boarded a canoe and according to Hawkeye's plan, headed north. They were not expecting any company. However, to their surprise, they saw a group of Hurons trailing them on a similar canoe. They chased off the followers by shooting down one of them. After canoeing for almost a day they finally reached their destination.

When they reached the northern shore, they disembarked and hid the canoe among the bushes and then set out for the rescue operation.

It was Uncas who found the trail of their enemies who took Alice, Cora and probably Gamut too. They also found the horses, which implied they had entered the Huron's territory. As they proceeded carefully, they saw a figure among the thicket near a pond. Hawkeye had almost shot him but just in time, the others saw it was Gamut in a native's attire and face paint.

The singer informed that Magua had made a plan to separate the two ladies. Alice was still with the Hurons while Cora was taken away to another camp. He added he was released after the Indians thought he was mentally unsound, always singing the psalms.

Heyward, disguised as a clown, accompanied Gamut and headed for Alice's rescue. Munro and Chingachgook left for the Delaware settlements to rescue Cora. Uncas and Hawkeye remained in the woods for any emergency.

A few Huron children saw Heyward and Gamut that raised an alarm and a few men rushed forward. Their plan was working so far, when the major pretended he was a French doctor. He told the men that he had come as a messenger and to treat the children. The Hurons believed him.

Before long, there were yelling outside that attracted everybody's attention. The Hurons had captured two tribes, who were tied to a pole. To Heyward's horror, one of them was Uncas.

When asked, Uncas replied he was pursuing a coward, a Huron who was standing alone. A simple reference to timidity was enough for the father to kill his son who had captured Uncas. However, the young Mohican was saved for the day. He was going to be executed the next morning.

When the crowd dispersed, the major looked for Alice in the area but in vain. Dusk was approaching. Meanwhile, a Huron warrior's wife was sick and he was called for treating her. Again, Heyward was horror-struck when he saw Magua, but the former guide could not recognize him in his disguise. Magua had identified Uncas and was insisting the Huron chief torture and kill the Mohican first thing in the morning.

When Heyward was led to a cavern where there was the sick woman, he found two things. One, Gamut was consoling her by singing; and two, the woman was visibly far beyond his powers of healing and was most likely to die.

As Heyward started checking the woman, the Huron chief asked the other women to leave. But the chief also left hurriedly after hearing the growl of a bear, leaving him alone with the woman.

It turned out to be Hawkeye in a bearskin! He explained how Munro and Chingachgook were in an old beaver lodge. And he had also found Alice on the other side of the cavern. In a jiffy, Heyward washed off his paint and they went to fetch the girl.

With his wicked smile, Magua appeared out of nowhere. When he saw the bear, he immediately knew it was fake, but the bear clasped him so tightly that he could hardly move.

The two men made a quick decision while Alice had fallen unconscious from fear. They had to leave by the entrance through which Magua had entered, but there was another obstacle. Some of the relatives of the sick woman were waiting outside.

Heyward covered Alice with the native woman's clothes and then told the Indians that he had to take the woman to the forest, where he was going to get the herbs. He added an evil spirit was lingering in the cavern. Hawkeye was following the duo from another side. The plan worked—Alice regained consciousness and they reached a safe distance. Then Hawkeye asked

Heyward and Alice to move towards the Delaware settlement while he went back to the Huron village, especially for Uncas.

So Hawkeye put on the bearskin and went back. He met Gamut, who was frightened seeing the bear. But Hawkeye signalled so that the singer could understand, and slowly he explained about Heyward and Alice and then the reason why he had returned.

'Can you lead me to him?' asked Hawkeye.

'The task will not be difficult,' said the singer.

They found Uncas in the middle of the village. Without losing a second, Uncas put on the bear costume, while Hawkeye put on Gamut's clothes while the singer dressed up like Uncas in his original attire. The Mohican and Hawkeye went passed the guards and reached the woods safely. Gamut was presumed to be safe considering the Hurons' attitude towards him as mentally unstable.

Moments later the duo heard a loud and long cry from the lodge where Uncas had been confined. Apparently the Hurons had discovered the escape but all they could see was Gamut singing the psalms. Hundreds of men had gathered; and they were, in fact, taken aback when Gamut started singing wildly. They also found the dead woman as well as Magua with his hands tied, who revealed that Hawkeye was still alive. This annoyed the Hurons terribly.

Without Alice, Magua had nothing with Cora, who was still captive. He pursued the hot-headed men to be careful, proving his leadership skills. But, while he was making this sacrifice to general considerations, Magua never lost sight of his motives.

The next morning he led a score of men—they were heading towards the Delaware camp. They knew their enemies had headed in that direction, as informed by the runners who were sent the previous night. As they proceeded, they saw a beaver but no one paid attention that the animal was watching their movements curiously. When they disappeared into the woods, Chingachgook appeared out of the beaver mask.

The band of Hurons arrived at the Delaware settlement with a friendly gesture. Cora was also in the hands of the Delawares, whose greatest orator, Hard Heart, greeted Magua and they talked about the recent developments. And the latter presented gifts with the loot from Fort William Henry. When Magua asked, the imprisoned woman was fine, and he surprised the Delawares when he told them that La Longue Carabine was in the settlement.

Through his demands, that an Indian-killer was in their company, he asked for the prisoners. A few moments later, from a lodge Cora, Alice,

Heyward and Hawkeye—but without Uncas—were called out before the gathering. The arms of the two sisters were entwined; the major was just behind them, and Hawkeye followed in the back.

A leader, Tamenund, who looked more than a hundred years old and had outlived three generations of warriors, appeared for the meeting. He was seated in the middle.

He asked, 'Which of the prisoners is La Longue Carabine?'

Heyward became protective and he claimed he was the notorious rifleman. Magua rejected it and thus they had a shooting contest as a proof of identity.

'You see that gourd hanging by the tree, major. If you are a marksman as you claim to be, let me see you break its shell!'

The gourd was one of the usual little vessels used by the Indians. It was suspended from a dead branch of a small pine, by a strip of deerskin, at the full distance of a hundred yards.

The major missed the shot but the real La Longue Carabine did not. But the hands of both the men were tied. Cora rushed and fell at the feet of Tamenund. Fortunately, she could convince him to hear from Uncas. Tamenund ordered to bring him to the circle.

The young Mohican came calmly, confidently.

'What language do you speak?' asked the leader.

'Like his fathers,' Uncas replied, 'with the tongue of a Delaware.'

Initially, Tamenund did not believe the Mohican's words. But when some of the Delaware tore the young man's hunting shirt, they could see a small tortoise tattoo in a bright blue tint on Uncas' chest.

The old man felt Uncas was a rebirth of his grandfather who was known by the same name and famed for courage during his youth. Thus, Uncas found a new power.

When Uncas was asked, he suggested all the captives should be freed and that none of them were real prisoners. In contrast to Magua's charge that Hawkeye was an Indian-killer, he protested that he never harmed a Delaware, but only the Hurons.

Soon, the Indian fled with Cora but not before Hawkeye

offered both, his rifle as well as life, for the bargain. He even proposed training the Hurons for shooting rifles, however, the villain was stubborn. Tamenund, with his ruling, made the matter worse.

The Hurons left triumphantly and they had even challenged Uncas and some of the Delaware to pursue them. Certainly, they were going to follow when the unspoken agreement was over. This lasted until certain length of the sun.

Uncas watched as Magua drove off with Cora. He went back and charted his course of action. Soon, he re-emerged to start a war ritual as a tribute to the god Manitou, the Great Spirit. Other followed him simultaneously.

They chanted, 'Manitou! Manitou! Manitou! Thou art great, thou art good, thou art wise: Manitou! Manitou! Thou art just. In the heavens, in the clouds, oh, I see many spots—many dark, many red: In the heavens, oh, I see many clouds.'

Meanwhile, Hawkeye sent a boy to fetch the rifles for him and Uncas that were hidden in the woods. The boy was wounded when some Hurons fired, but they were chased off quickly. Shortly they were about to leave for the campaign.

Uncas and Hawkeye divided twenty warriors each among themselves. Heyward was asked to lead but he declined and rather volunteered to help Hawkeye. They held a secret conference in the woods and they were going to attack from two directions. Everything was set for the assault.

Among the woods, a figure appeared and he was almost mistaken to be a Huron and shot when it was realized that the man was Gamut, the singer, who was still disguised as an Indian. This was the second time he might have been hit by a bullet! He had information on where Cora was held captive in the Huron camp.

The first gunfire started near the pond where Chingachgook had appeared as a beaver. The Hurons were defeated without much effort. In a way, the attacking parties from both sides were evenly matched.

Uncas and his band were the first to see Magua. He was riding on a passage that led to the mountain. The men saw a fluttering white robe.

'It is Cora!' said Heyward, who was equally horrified and delighted.

'Cora! Cora!' said Uncas.

'It is the maiden!' Hawkeye joined in. 'Courage, lady; we come! We come!'

On the other side, a few moments later, Magua was offering Cora his rest house or his knife. She was unwilling as always. The man raised his knife but hesitated; and he was surprised when Uncas sprang forward.

Incidentally, a Huron stabbed Cora on the chest while Magua jabbed Uncas with a tomahawk on his back. Out of nowhere, Hawkeye appeared and shot Magua, who died on the spot.

The next day was a day of mourning for the Delawares. Chingachgook was silent. Munro was grief-stricken, sitting at the foot of his daughter. Gamut was singing as usual. And the people were paying homage to the two dead bodies.

Tamenund told the gathering, 'The face of the Manitou is behind a cloud! His eye is turned from you; His ears are shut; His tongue gives no answer. You see Him not; yet His judgments are before you. Let your hearts be open and your spirits tell no lie.'

Then Chingachgook said he was all alone but Hawkeye interrupted, 'The gifts of our colours may be different, but God has so placed us as to journey in the same path. I have no kin, and I may also say, like you, no people.'

They held their hands in the name of friendship. Tamenund said, 'I have lived to see the last warrior of the wise race of the Mohicans.'

The Legend of Sleepy Hollow

Washington Irving

On the eastern shore of the Hudson River, there lies a small market town or rural port. Some call it Greensburgh, but it is popularly known by the name of Tarry Town. We are told that this name was given in the older days by the good housewives of the country close by, because their husbands loitered about in the village on market days.

About two miles away, there is a little valley among high hills, which is one of the quietest places in the whole world. The people in the valley have a strange character, and are descendants from the original Dutch settlers. The place has long been known by the name of Sleepy Hollow, and its rustic lads are called the Sleepy Hollow Boys throughout all the neighbouring country.

A drowsy, dreamy influence seems to hang over the land. Some say that the place was bewitched by a High German doctor, during the

early days of the settlement; others, that an old Indian chief, the prophet or wizard of his tribe, held his private meetings there before the country was discovered by Master Hendrick Hudson. It seems quite certain that the place still continues under the sway of some witching power that holds a spell over the minds of the good people.

The Hollow is the Headless Horseman, presumed as the ghost of a Hessian trooper who had his head shot by a stray cannonball during an anonymous battle of the American Revolutionary War.

It is remarkable that this illusion is not confined to the native inhabitants of the valley, but is unconsciously imbibed by everyone who resides there for a time.

In this by-place of nature there stayed, in a remote period of American history, that is to say, some thirty years ago, Ichabod Crane, an inhabitant of Connecticut, for the purpose of instructing the children of the locality.

The surname of Crane well suited this person. He had long arms and legs with narrow shoulders. His feet were large, and his head was small. His eyes were green and wide, and his nose looked like a beak of a bird. His clothes were too big and blew around him when he moved, and his way of walking was awkward.

Overall, he was a careful man, and ever bore in mind the golden maxim, 'Spare the rod and spoil the child.' Ichabod Crane's scholars certainly were not spoiled.

I would not have it imagined, however, that he was one of those cruel dictators of the school who take joy in the smart of their subjects. On the contrary, he administered justice with discrimination rather than severity; taking the burden off the backs of the weak, and laying it on those of the strong. When not at school, Ichabod would join the somewhat older boys in his class, and on special occasions, he would accompany home the younger ones who had pretty sisters or talented mothers in the kitchen.

To these ends, he stayed on somewhat good terms with his students, especially when a good meal was at stake. Ichabod had a voracious appetite. He ate huge

volumes of food, contradictory to the indications of his bony frame.

He assisted the farmers occasionally in the lighter labours of their farms, helped to make food, mended the fences, took the horses to water, drove the cows from pasture and cut wood for the winter fire. He laid aside, too, all the dignity and absolute sway with which he lorded in his little empire, the school, and became wonderfully gentle. He knew how to endear himself to mothers by tending to their small children.

Offering services to his patrons was not the only secondary occupation this teacher possessed, but he was also a choirmaster and music instructor to a private few. Ichabod proudly stood in church, leading the others in psalms. Certain it was, his voice resounded far above all the rest of the congregation; and there are peculiar quavers still to be heard in that church, and which may even be heard half a mile off, quite to the opposite side of the mill-pond, on a still Sunday morning, which are said to be legitimately descended from the nose of Ichabod Crane.

The schoolmaster was generally a man of some importance in the female circle of a rural neighbourhood; being considered a kind of idle, gentleman-like personage. Our man of letters, therefore, was peculiarly happy in the smiles of all the country damsels.

How he would figure among them in the churchyard, between services on Sundays; gathering grapes for them from the wild vines that overran the surrounding trees; reciting for their amusement all the epitaphs on the tombstones; or sauntering, with a whole bevy of them, along the banks of the adjacent mill-pond; while the more bashful country bumpkins hung sheepishly back, envying his superior elegance and position.

He was also a kind of travelling gazette, carrying the whole budget of local gossip from house to house, so that his appearance was always greeted with satisfaction. Most women respected him as a man of great wisdom because he had read several books, and was a perfect master of Cotton Mather's *History of New England Witchcraft*, in which he most firmly believed.

In fact, he was the combination of small cunning and simple innocence. He was very hungry and his digesting power was extraordinary.

His only resource, either to drown thought or drive away evil spirits, was to sing psalm tunes and the good people of Sleepy Hollow, as they sat by their doors of an evening, were often filled with awe at hearing his nasal melody, 'in linked sweetness long drawn out,' floating from the distant hill, or along the dusky road.

Another of his sources of fearful pleasure was to pass long winter evenings with the Old Dutch wives, who told regional tales which were often marvellous. In turn, he would tell stories of signs and visions from his native Connecticut.

The way home from these story-laden evenings would, however, prey upon the imagination of this country instructor. Ichabod imagined haunting, shrouded, snowy figures out of nature. Ichabod's greatest fear was to, perhaps, encounter the Galloping Hessian, the Headless

Horseman. His every step anticipated this chance meeting.

All these, however, were mere terrors of the night, phantoms of the mind that walked in darkness.

He had seen many illusions in his time, yet daylight put an end to all these evils; when his path was crossed by a lady, Katrina Van Tassel, who came in the church once a week to learn Ichabod's instructions in psalms.

Katrina was the only daughter of a wealthy Dutch farmer. She was eighteen years old and plump as a partridge. She wore beautiful dresses, and ornaments of pure gold, which her great grandmother had brought over from Saardam.

Her father, Old Baltus Van Tassel was a very successful, happy and liberal-hearted farmer. His home was situated on the banks of the Hudson.

Ichabod was surprised to see such luxury. His craving grew from food to wealth.

In his imagination he was thinking about the meadowlands, the rich fields of wheat, of rye, of buckwheat, and Indian corn, and the orchards burdened with ruddy fruit, which surrounded the warm residence of Van Tassel. He wanted to marry Katrina because she was the only child of her father and through her he could get all these luxuries. To win her heart was difficult because she was a flirt and she was popular amongst many.

He was ready to compete with anyone in this regard. One such competitor was Brom Van Brunt, the hero of the country. He had broad shoulders and curly hair. Van Brunt was fit and fun loving. Because of his strength, he was referred to as Brom Bones, and his competitors loyally followed him.

This hero had for some time singled out Katrina for the object of his uncouth gallantries, and though his amorous toying was something like the gentle caresses and endearments of a bear, yet it was whispered that she did not altogether discourage his hopes. Certainly, his advances were signals for rival candidates to retire. Such was the kind of rival with whom Ichabod Crane had to compete, and, considering, all things, a stouter man than he would have shrunk from the competition, and a wiser man would have despaired.

However, Ichabod was not carried away by Brom Bones. Ichabod pursued Katrina, even under the doting eye of her protective father. Brom Bones wanted to settle this issue with brute force, but our gentle school teacher knew his challenger and chose less aggressive means to battle for the fair maiden. Ichabod became the object of whimsical persecution to Bones and his gang of rough riders. They smoked out his singing-school by blocking the chimney, broke into the schoolhouse at night, and turned everything topsy-turvy, so that the poor schoolmaster began to think all the witches in the country held their meetings there.

But what was still more annoying, Brom took all opportunities of ridiculing him in the presence of his mistress.

In this way, matters went on for some time, without producing any material effect on the relative situations of the challenging powers. On a fine autumnal afternoon, Ichabod, in pensive mood, sat on the tall stool from where he usually watched all the concerns of his little literary realm.

Apparently there had been some appalling act of justice recently inflicted, for his scholars were all busily intent upon their books, or slyly whispering behind them with one eye kept upon the master; and a kind of buzzing stillness reigned throughout the schoolroom.

It was suddenly interrupted by the appearance of a boy in tow-cloth jacket and trousers. Van Tassel had sent the boy with the message for Ichabod that Van Tassel invited him home for a party. After he had received this message, there was shuffling in the quiet classroom.

Ichabod sent the students home early. He was very excited. He took at least an extra half hour at his toilet, bracing up at his best.

He dressed up perfectly. He wanted to make his best appearance in front of the beautiful Katrina. He even borrowed a horse from the neighbour, Hans Van Ripper who was a rich farmer. The animal was an old plough horse. He was thin and shagged, and had a head like a hammer; his rusty mane and tail were tangled and knotted with burs; one of his eyes had lost its pupil, and was glaring and spectral, but the other had the gleam of a genuine devil in it.

His name was Gunpowder; although he was old and docile, and was so

named for his quick discharge in the event of another horse of the opposite sex or whatever moved his fancy. He had, in fact, been a favourite steed of his master, the choleric Van Ripper, who was a furious rider, and had infused, very probably, some of his own spirit into the animal. Ichabod was very happy to get a horse because he wanted to go to the castle of Van Tassel like a proper gentleman.

Astride this horse, Ichabod cut a comical appearance, resembling a gawky bird, with his angled limbs protruding awkwardly. Ichabod was a suitable figure for such a steed.

He put the saddle on Gunpowder, and sat on him. He put his feet into the stirrups and began to ride. He had a whip in his hand; he had a hat on his head and his long black coat fluttered almost to the horse's tail.

Ichabod was moving very slowly on the horse through the forest and enjoying every movement of the jolly autumn nature. He was thinking about Katrina, and that all would be good.

At last, Ichabod arrived at the castle of Heer Van Tassel in the evening. The castle was decorated very well from outside. When he entered into the castle, he was surprised to see the interior decoration; it was even more beautiful.

He was looking all around. He noticed that many rich people had been invited to the party. He met with Van Tassel who introduced him to other people. The men, women and their children were looking presentable, beautiful and charming. The men wore coats, pants and polished shoes. Ladies wore long gowns and hats.

Ichabod saw Brom Bones, who was the hero of this party. He rode his horse named Daredevil, which was full of mettle and mischief and could not be controlled by anyone except Brom Bones.

After an introduction with guests, Ichabod entered the parlour room where he saw many delicious dishes, which were decorated on the dining table. He gazed at these different types of dishes. It was the first time in his life that he saw such a variety of dishes, and his mouth began to water. There were sweet cakes and short cakes, ginger cakes and honey cakes, and the whole family of cakes.

Besides, there were apple pies, and peach pies, and pumpkin pies, slices of ham, smoked beef; and moreover delectable dishes of preserved plums, and peaches, and pears, and quinces; not to mention broiled shad and roasted chickens, together with bowls of milk and cream, all mingled higgledy-piggledy. The dinner was indeed extraordinary.

Ichabod continued to stare at the unimaginable luxury and splendour. Then, he decided to go back to his schoolhouse some time later.

Old Baltus Van Tassel was very happy and his hospitable attentions were brilliant. It was the time to enjoy dancing. Therefore, Van Tassel requested the guests to reach the dance room. The sound of the music could be heard and all the guests reached the common room.

There was the musician, who had been the itinerant orchestra of the neighbourhood for more than half a century. His instrument was also old and battered as he was himself.

The greater part of the time he scraped on two or three strings, accompanying every movement of the bow with a motion of the head; bowing almost to the ground, and stamping with his foot whenever a fresh couple were to start.

All were dancing in pairs. Children too enjoyed themselves. Finally Ichabod came to dance with lovely Katrina Van Tassel on the dance floor. He was very happy. She was also smiling and kept talking to him. On the other hand Brom Bones, was staring at them with jealousy.

After dancing, Old Van Tassel sat smoking at one end of the piazza, and while speaking of old times, the men shared stories of battle and bravery.

The British and American lines had run near it during the war; it had, therefore, been the scene of marauding and infested with refugees, cowboys and all kinds of border chivalry.

Just sufficient time had elapsed to enable each storyteller to dress up his tale with a little becoming fiction, and, in the indistinctness of his recollection, to make himself the hero of every exploit.

There was the story of Doffue Martling, a large blue-bearded Dutchman, who had nearly taken a British frigate with an old iron nine-pounder from a mud breastwork only that his gun burst at the sixth discharge.

And there was an old gentleman who shall be nameless, being too rich to be lightly mentioned. Being an excellent master of defence, he had fought the Battle of White Plains.

There were several more that had been equally great in the field, not one of whom but was persuaded that he had a considerable hand in bringing the war to a happy termination.

These tales were followed by the exchange of ghost stories. The Sleepy Hollow was the place of dreams and fancies. Several of the Sleepy Hollow people were present at the party and, as usual, were doling out their wild and wonderful legends.

Many dismal tales were told about funeral trains, and mourning cries and wailings heard and seen about the great tree where the unfortunate Major Andre was taken, and which stood in the neighbourhood.

Some mention was made also of the woman in white that haunted the dark glen at Raven Rock, and was often heard shrieking on winter nights before a storm, having perished there in the snow.

The story that dominated all the rest, of course, was that of the Headless Horseman. According to legend, his horse was in the churchyard each night. The church, white in colour, was situated on a small rounded hill, which was surrounded by lots of tall trees. On one side of the church extended a wide woody dell, the Hudson run through the broken rocks and trunks of fallen trees.

The green layer of grass looked very nice. Some miles away from the church, there was a bridge, which was also surrounded by long trees, which gave a fearful darkness during the nighttime.

This bridge was made from wood and was the favourite place of the Headless Horseman, where he was mostly encountered.

The tale was told of old Brouwer, a most heretical disbeliever in ghosts, how he met the Horseman returning from his foray into Sleepy Hollow, and was obliged to get up behind him; how they galloped over bush and brake, over hill and swamp, until they reached the bridge; when the Horseman suddenly turned into a skeleton, threw old Brouwer into the brook, and sprang away over the treetops with a clap of thunder.

Brom Bones added his own experience of racing on Daredevil. He told the listeners that one night when he was returning to his home from the neighbouring village of Sing Sing, he happened to encounter Headless Horseman.

He had offered to race with him for a bowl of punch, and should have won it too, for Daredevil beat the goblin horse all hollow, but just as they came to the church bridge, the Hessian bolted, and vanished in a flash of fire.

All listeners were hearing these horror tales. Hair-raising tales of sounds and phenomena mesmerised Ichabod, who later shared his own personal experiences of the supernatural powers. He repaid them in kind with large extracts from his invaluable author, Cotton Mather, and added many marvellous events that had taken place in his native state of Connecticut, and fearful sights, which he had seen, in his nightly walks about Sleepy Hollow.

It was dark when the party broke up, the bewitching time of night. The old farmers gathered together their families in their wagons, and were heard for some time rattling along the hollow roads, and over the distant hills.

Ichabod did not immediately notice because he had sadly left the party. Ichabod and Katrina had conversed before he left, and the man had walked away from the evening looking sad. As he was returning to his schoolhouse, it was a very dark and fearful night. He was already feeling uncomfortable after listening to ghost stories. The hour was as dismal as he was himself.

Far below him the Tappan Zee spread its dusky and indistinct waste of waters, with here and there the tall mast of a sloop, riding quietly at anchor under the land. He was only hearing the barking of the watchdog from the opposite side of the Hudson River. He could hardly notice the distance due to dark and dusty night. But he was surely away from the farmhouse.

He did not hear any sound. No signs of life occurred near or around him, but suddenly he heard the voice of a cricket and frog

The voice of the frog was coming from the marsh. The stories of ghosts and goblins, which he had heard in the party, were crowding upon his mind. The night was growing dark and because of the cloudy sky, the stars were not clearly visible.

He was feeling lonely. Whenever he looked at the tall trees and dense bushes, the scenes of ghosts appeared in his mind. The tall trees were looking like ghosts. But he kept on moving forward without turning back. It was not too long, however, before the teacher realised the potential danger of time and place.

When he arrived at the centre of the road, he saw an enormous tulip tree. It was unusually larger than other trees. He was shivering with fear. It was connected with the tragical story of the unfortunate Andre, who had been taken prisoner; and was universally known by the name of Major Andre's tree. The common people regarded it with a mixture of respect and superstition, partly out of sympathy, and partly from the tales of strange sights, and doleful lamentations, narrated about it.

He went closer to the tree and began to whistle. He thought that somebody would hear his voice and answer. But he did not get any reply. Suddenly he heard a groan—his teeth chattered, and his knees smote against the saddle: it was but the rubbing of one huge bough upon another, as the breeze swayed them about. He passed the tree in safety, but new perils were lying before him.

About 200 yards from the tree, a small brook crossed the road, and ran into a marshy and thickly wooded glen, known by the name of Wiley's Swamp. There was a small bridge over this stream. On that side of the road where the brook entered the wood, a group of oaks and chestnuts, matted thick with wild grapevines, threw a cavernous gloom over it.

To pass this bridge was the severest trial. It was at this spot that the unfortunate Andre was captured, and under the covert of those chestnuts and vines were the sturdy yeomen concealed who surprised him. This has ever since been considered a haunted stream, and fearful are the feelings of the schoolboy who has to pass it alone after the dark. When Ichabod and his horse, Gunpowder, approached the stream's bridge, he tried to steer the horse ahead, but the stubborn animal resisted and went its own way, directing Ichabod into some bushes.

Ichabod tried to whip the horse onward, and Gunpowder leapt ahead, only to stop abruptly when Ichabod sighted a large figure. He wanted to return to his schoolhouse. But there was no way to do so. He could hardly get his power and asked this giant figure who he was, but he did not get any reply. Due to darkness he could not see him clearly. The hair of the affrighted schoolteacher rose upon his head with terror. He repeated his demand in a still more agitated voice. Still there was no answer.

Once more, he nudged the sides of the inflexible Gunpowder, and, shutting his eyes, broke forth with involuntary fervour into a psalm tune. Just then the shadowy object of alarm put itself in motion, and with a scramble and a bound stood at once in the middle of the road. Though the night was dark, yet the form of the unknown in some degree could be ascertained.

He appeared to be a horseman of large dimensions, and mounted on a black horse of powerful frame. He made no offer of molestation or sociability, but kept aloof on one side of the road, jogging along on the blind side of old Gunpowder, who had now got over his fright and waywardness.

When Ichabod came upon a more open area, he was able to view his travelling companion. It appeared to be the Headless Horseman, with a head riding on the saddle. Ichabod tried to spur Gunpowder to flee, but the other rider kept up with them. They had now reached the road, which turns off to Sleepy Hollow; but Gunpowder, who seemed possessed with a demon, instead of keeping up with it, made an opposite turn, and plunged headlong downhill to the left.

This road leads through a sandy hollow shaded by trees for about a quarter of a mile, where it crosses the bridge famous in the goblin story; and just beyond swells the green knoll on which stands the whitewashed church. It

was there Ichabod hoped to lead the Headless Horseman so his pursuit would stop by the bridge. Unfortunately, though, in so desperately riding the horse, Gunpowder's saddle fell off, and Ichabod held on for life.

This did not deter Ichabod from reaching that bridge, yet when his approach seemed certain, the Headless Horseman rose in his saddle and threw the head at Ichabod. It hit the teacher's head, knocking him to the ground.

The next morning the old horse was found without his saddle, and with the bridle under his feet, soberly cropping the grass at his master's gate. Ichabod did not make his appearance at breakfast; dinner-hour came, but there was still no sign of him. The boys assembled at the schoolhouse, but in vain. Hans Van Ripper now began to feel uneasy about the fate of poor Ichabod, and his saddle. An inquiry was set on foot, and after diligent investigation they came upon his traces. In one part of the road leading to the church was found the saddle trampled in the dirt; the tracks of horses' hoofs deeply dented in the road, and evidently at furious speed, were traced to the bridge, beyond which, on the bank of a broad part of the brook, where the water ran deep and black, was found the hat of the unfortunate Ichabod, and close beside it a shattered pumpkin.

The brook was searched, but the body of the schoolmaster was not to be discovered. Hans Van Ripper as executor of his estate, examined the bundle which contained all his worldly effects. They consisted of two shirts and a half; two stocks for the neck; a pair or two of worsted stockings; an old pair of corduroy small-clothes; a rusty razor; a book of psalm tunes full of dog's ears; and a broken pitch-pipe. As to the books and furniture of the schoolhouse, they belonged to the community, excepting Cotton Mather's *History of New England Witchcraft*, and a book of dreams and fortune-telling; in which last was a sheet of foolscap much scribbled and blotted in several fruitless attempts to make a copy of verses in honour of the heiress of Van Tassel. These magic books and the poetic scrawl were consigned to flames by Hans Van Ripper; who, from that time forward, determined to send his children no more to school, observing that he never knew any good come of this same reading and writing. Whatever money the schoolmaster possessed, and he had received his quarter's pay but a day or two before, he must have had about his person at the time of his disappearance.

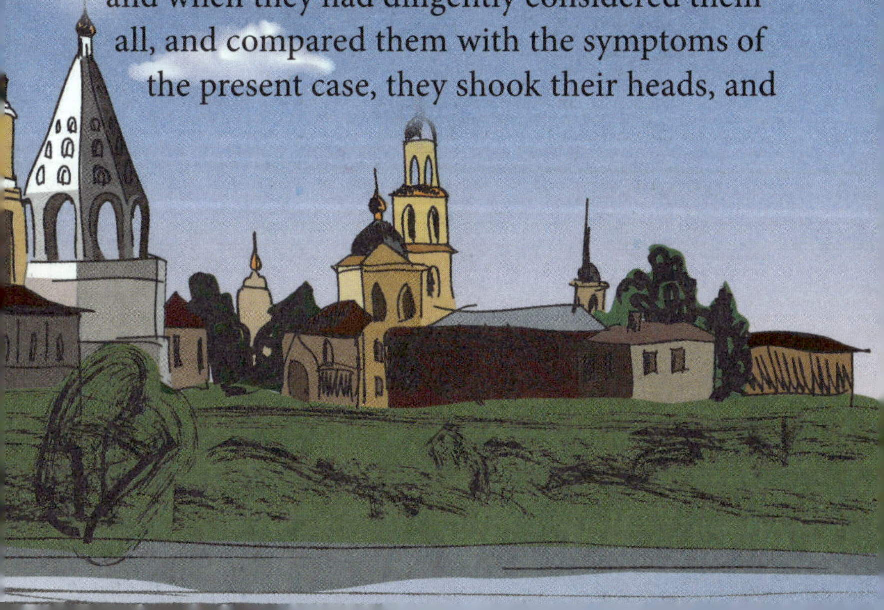

With time, it came to be believed that the Headless Horseman carried Ichabod away, and since he had neither money nor family, he was quickly forgotten. The mysterious event caused much speculation at the church on the following Sunday. Knots of gazers and gossips were collected in the churchyard, at the bridge, and at the spot where the hat and pumpkin had been found. The stories of Brouwer, of Bones, and a whole budget of others were called to mind; and when they had diligently considered them all, and compared them with the symptoms of the present case, they shook their heads, and came to the conclusion that Ichabod had been carried off by the Galloping Hessian.

As he was a bachelor, and in nobody's debt, nobody troubled his head any more about him. The school was shifted to a different quarter of the Hollow. An old farmer, who had been down to New York on a visit several years after, and from whom this account of the ghostly adventure was received, brought home the intelligence that Ichabod Crane was still alive; that he had left the neighbourhood partly through fear of the goblin and Hans Van Ripper, and partly in mortification at having been suddenly

dismissed by the heiress; that he had changed his quarters to a distant part of the country; had kept school and studied law at the same time; had been admitted to the bar; turned politician; electioneered; written for the newspapers; and finally had been made a justice of the Ten Pound Court. Brom Bones, too, who, shortly after his rival's disappearance conducted the blooming Katrina in triumph to the altar, was observed to look exceedingly knowing whenever the story of Ichabod was related, and always burst into a hearty laugh at the mention of the pumpkin; which led some to suspect that he knew more about the matter than he chose to tell.

The old country wives, however, who are the best judges of these matters, maintain to this day that Ichabod was spirited away by supernatural means; and it is a favourite story often told about the neighbourhood round the winter evening fire. The bridge became more than ever an object of superstitious awe; and that may be the reason why the road has been altered of late years, so as to approach the church by the border of the millpond. The schoolhouse being deserted soon fell to decay, and was reported to be haunted by the ghost of the unfortunate schoolmaster. The ploughboy, loitering homeward of a still summer evening, has often fancied his voice at a distance, chanting a melancholy psalm tune among the tranquil solitudes of Sleepy Hollow.

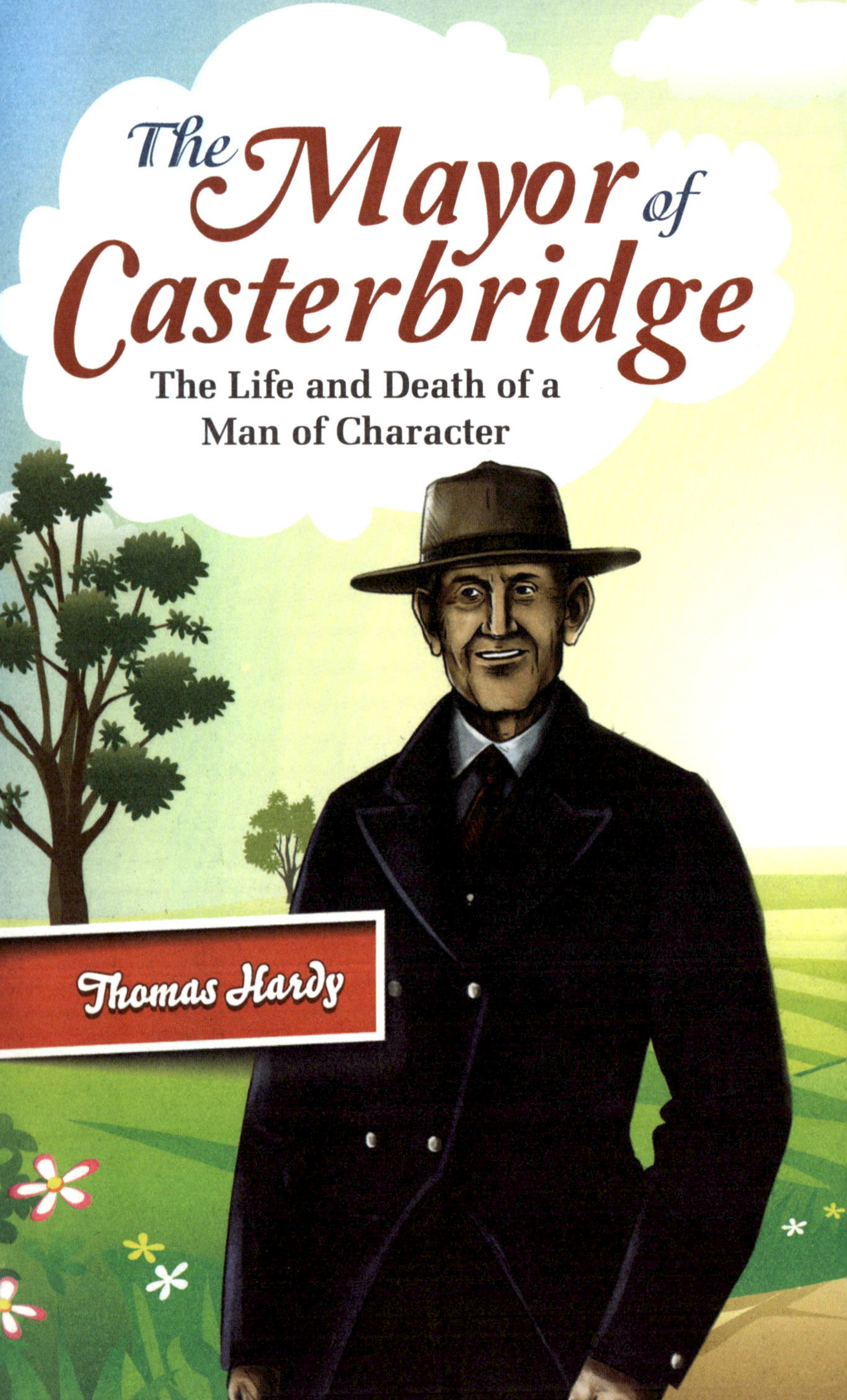
The Mayor of Casterbridge
The Life and Death of a
Man of Character
Thomas Hardy

It was a summer evening, in the first half of the nineteenth century. Michael Henchard, a young and unemployed hay-trusser, was walking across the town of Weydon-Priors in Upper Wessex. His wife, Susan—who was also carrying their infant daughter, Elizabeth—accompanied him. They had been walking for a long time and it was evident from the pale layer of dust on their scraggy clothes.

The twenty-one-year-old trusser and his family came across a fair in the town, where they halted for some refreshments and drinks. Henchard drank some rum, which was going to change his life forever. In a drunken rage, he told the crowd that he was auctioning his wife and daughter off.

At five guineas, a sailor agreed to buy the wife and the baby and took them away. Meanwhile, Henchard passed out from excessive drinking.

The next morning when he woke up, he was distraught to find that he had sold off his wife and daughter. He found the money in his pocket but was furious that Susan had left him.

Henchard resolved to find them. He started by visiting a church, where he took an oath:

'I, Michael Henchard, on this morning of the sixteenth of September, do take an oath before God that I will avoid all liquors for the space of twenty-one years to come, being a year for every year that I have lived.'

He went on searching for a few months until he reached one seaport. There he found that some persons matching the description of his family had emigrated a little time before. He decided to stop his futile search and rather leave for the town of Casterbridge.

Eighteen years had elapsed when the story unfolded again.

The roads leading to the town of Weydon-Priors was dusty as always. Nevertheless, the people had changed entirely. Susan Henchard was wearing a mourning dress then. From the view, it was not hard to tell her companion was her grown-up daughter, Elizabeth.

'Why did we come here?' asked the daughter.

'My dear Elizabeth,' explained the other who called herself Mrs Newson, 'it was here I first met with Newson—on such a day as this. And it was here that I last saw the relation we are going to look for—Mr Michael Henchard.'

On one hand, Mr Richard Newson, the sailor who bought them was presumably dead, as he had disappeared in a sea journey. However, the mother, on the other, had not told her daughter much about Henchard but only about being a mere blood relative.

The older woman found upon queries from the townspeople that Michael Henchard had gone to Casterbridge. The ladies lodged at Weydon-Priors for the night and left for the town the following morning.

For eighteen years, the Newsons had been living in Canada. Susan had tried a couple of time to reveal the truth but she had been dismissing it, for the sake of her daughter's security.

Before long, they reached Casterbridge and came across two men, engaged in an argumentative conversation.

Elizabeth spoke first.

'Why do those men mentioned the name of Henchard in their talk—the name of our relative?'

'I thought so too,' replied Mrs Henchard-Newson.

'That seems a hint to us that he is still here.'

'Yes.'

'Shall I run after them, and ask them about him.'

'No, no, no! He may be in the workhouse, or in the stocks, for all we know.'

They came across the King's Arm, which was one of the best restaurants in Casterbridge. Outside, the common people were gathering while the elites of the town were having a sumptuous meal in the restaurant. The fine wine and dine gathering was visible through a spacious bay window.

The younger lady asked a passer-by, 'What's going on tonight?'

'Well, you must be a stranger sure,' the passer-by replied, 'It's a great public dinner of the gentle-people—that's Mr Henchard, the Mayor of Casterbridge, at the end of the table, that's the Council men right and left. . .'

'Henchard!' Elizabeth was visibly surprised.

'I don't think I can ever meet Mr Henchard. He is not how I thought he would be—he overpowers me! I don't wish to see him anymore.'

Susan surprised her daughter more with her sudden change of mind. Then, they overheard and learnt a couple of things about Michael Henchard. First, the mayor had

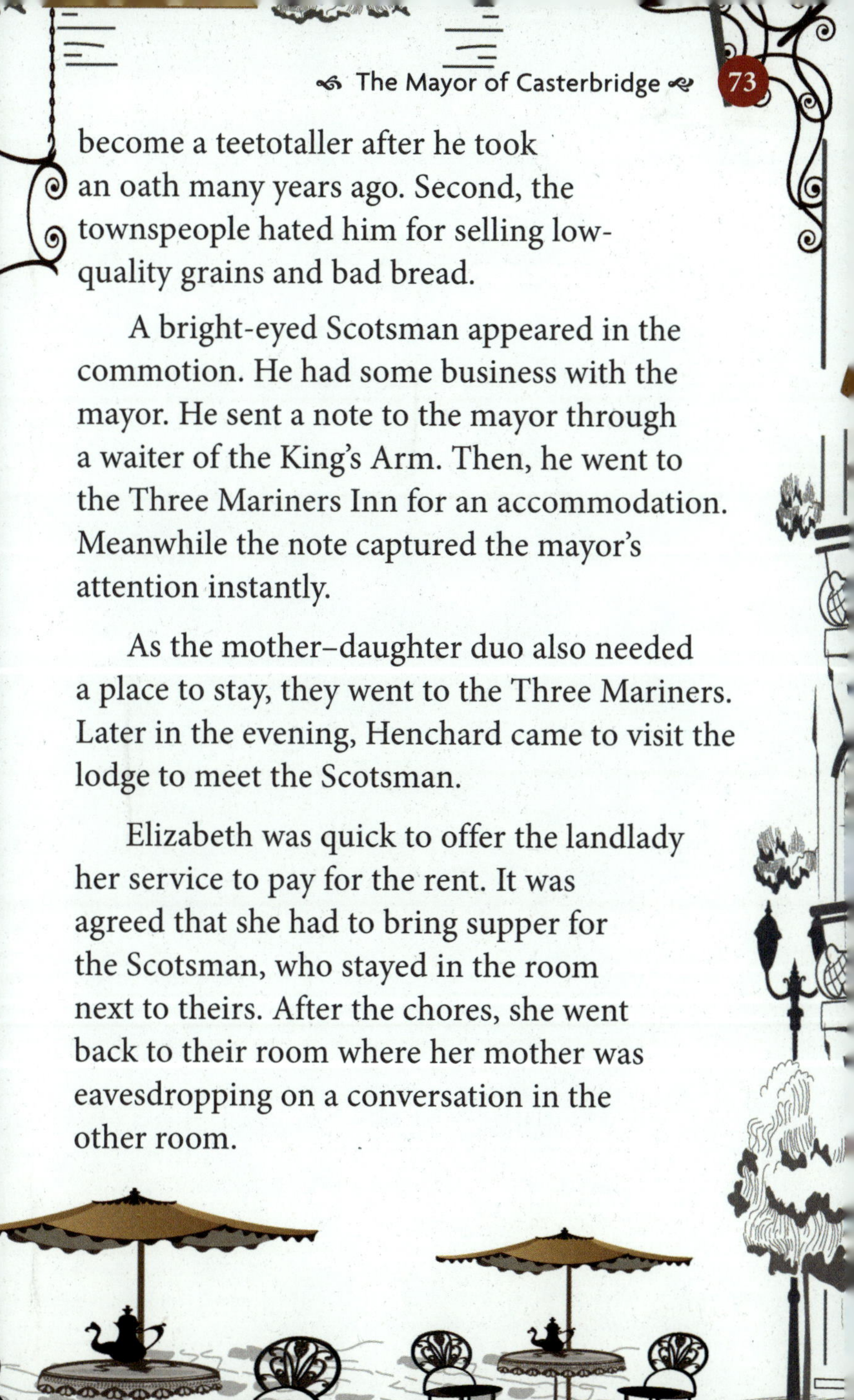

become a teetotaller after he took an oath many years ago. Second, the townspeople hated him for selling low-quality grains and bad bread.

A bright-eyed Scotsman appeared in the commotion. He had some business with the mayor. He sent a note to the mayor through a waiter of the King's Arm. Then, he went to the Three Mariners Inn for an accommodation. Meanwhile the note captured the mayor's attention instantly.

As the mother–daughter duo also needed a place to stay, they went to the Three Mariners. Later in the evening, Henchard came to visit the lodge to meet the Scotsman.

Elizabeth was quick to offer the landlady her service to pay for the rent. It was agreed that she had to bring supper for the Scotsman, who stayed in the room next to theirs. After the chores, she went back to their room where her mother was eavesdropping on a conversation in the other room.

She found that the Scotsman was named Donald Farfrae, who was on his way to the United States. He made a convincing suggestion to Mr Henchard on how to upgrade the wheat to wholesome quality. The mayor was thrilled and offered a job but Farfrae declined.

'I need to get a manager desperately,' said Henchard.

'I wish I could stay—sincerely I would like to,' Farfrae replied. 'But no—it cannot be! I want to see the world.'

Later, Elizabeth was called to run errands for the inn. She was apparently attracted to Farfrae, who sang and entertained the crowd at the inn. Mr Henchard went away disappointed.

The next morning, Elizabeth was sad to see, through the window, Farfrae leaving the inn. Henchard accompanied him and the men walked down the street.

Her mother had some other plans. Later in the day, she sent Elizabeth to give a note to

Mr Henchard that if he wanted to see a couple of distant relatives, who were in town, he should write a note back. If not, they would leave Casterbridge as quietly as possible.

When Elizabeth reached Henchard's office, she was shocked to find Farfrae sitting inside though he did not recognize her. Incidentally, in the morning, Henchard had re-offered the Scotsman to name his terms and finally won him over.

When Farfrae went to fetch Henchard for the guest, Elizabeth saw a man going inside the mayor's chamber.

'Joshua Jopp, sir—by appointment—the new manager,' she heard the newcomer's voice from the room.

'The new manager—he's in his office!' Henchard said.

'In his office?'

'I mentioned Thursday. And as you did not keep your appointment, I have appointed another manager.'

'You said Thursday or Saturday, sir,' Jopp begged.

'I am sorry for you. But it can't be helped.' Henchard concluded.

Elizabeth saw the man coming out, with anger written all over his face. She entered the room immediately. The man read her note and could not hide his astonishment.

Immediately he learnt that Mr Newson was no more. All he could do was to write a note back to Susan:

'Meet me at eight this evening, if you can, at the Ring. The place is easy to find. I can say no more now. The news upsets me almost. The girl seems to be in ignorance. Keep her so until I have seen you.—MH'

Henchard handed a symbolic amount of five guineas to Elizabeth too—the same amount Newson had paid him—but he did not mention about it.

The Ring at Casterbridge was one of the finest Roman amphitheatres in the country, set just off the main road. It had a grim history as a place for execution. It was also huge and dark, offering a perfect location for secret meetings.

Soon the couple reached the place on time. In the middle of the arena, none of them spoke at first. Then Susan leant against Henchard, who supported her in his arms.

'I don't drink,' the man's first few words were in a deeply apologetic tone. 'You hear, Susan?—I don't drink now—I haven't since that night.'

Henchard told her how he searched for her and the daughter. And Susan explained how she owed Newson who took him as his wife. The man could not control his sentiments, 'Ts-s-s! How could you be so simple?'

'I don't know. Yet it would have been very wicked—if I had not thought like that!' cried Susan.

They had no time to lose but they needed to put the things on a priority basis. There were many other things at stake, including Elizabeth's future and the mayor's reputation.

So they made a plan: Henchard was to give Susan sufficient money to rent a cottage on High Street. They were going to pretend to fall in love and remarry, while taking in Elizabeth as a stepdaughter.

When Henchard reached home, he confided the entire family story to Farfrae. The manager suggested his employer should make amends to Susan. Then Henchard also disclosed about Lucetta Templeman, a young lady from Jersey who had helped him when he was sick during a journey. He had even planned to marry her but things had changed then. And as requested, Farfrae agreed to write a letter to the lady to break up their relationship.

According to the plan, Susan moved into a cottage, located in the western part of the town, with her daughter. There Henchard would often go and visit Susan, which unsurprisingly became a talk of the town. It was indeed more baffling how such a successful mayor had fallen for Susan, a sickly woman who some of the townspeople nicknamed her as 'The Ghost' for her pale complexion.

On one windless November morning, Michael Henchard remarried Susan and Farfrae was the groomsman.

As months passed, Elizabeth was becoming prettier. She was also becoming more popular in the town; so was Donald Farfrae, though there was still no visible attraction between the two.

On the other hand, Henchard was as always going on his way. He had a fight with Farfrae over the conduct of Abel Whittle, another employee who was frequently late for his work.

The tension somehow sank in and then came a celebration of a national event. Farfrae approached his employer to lend him some rick-clothes to himself and a few others.

Henchard was in a good mood; he agreed, 'Have as many clothes as you like.'

On the day of the celebration, a heavy rainfall destroyed the festive spirit in one corner of the town that was organised by the mayor. However, on the other side, Farfrae had used the rick-clothes to make a tent that not only attracted the townspeople but also make the event a grand success. When Henchard visited the tent, he saw Farfrae was dancing with his daughter. To make it worse, some folks dared say that Farfrae would surpass his master.

'No,' Henchard was grumpy. 'He won't be that, because he's going to leave me soon.'

Henchard was not thinking about the consequences at all. Things reached such a height that Henchard dictated Elizabeth to stop speaking with Farfrae, which she did obediently. However, the manager had opened his own business and had been successful as well. No wonder Henchard was frustrated beyond imagination, even if Farfrae never considered himself as a competitor to his former boss.

Meanwhile Susan's health was deteriorating. Elizabeth did her best to nurse her mother. She asked her daughter to do her a favour. She wrote a letter and addressed to Michael Henchard, who was not supposed to open it until Elizabeth's wedding day. Shortly, she passed away.

One morning, Henchard received a letter from Lucetta who he used to court before reuniting with his family. She wrote that she would be passing Casterbridge but she did not turn up on the scheduled day.

A couple of weeks later Henchard finally decided to tell the truth. He called in Elizabeth.

'What did your mother tell you about me—my history?' he began.

'That you were related by marriage,' Elizabeth said.

'She should have told you more—before you knew me!' He gathered all his strength and continued, 'Your mother and I were man and wife when we were young. What you saw was our second marriage. Your mother was too honest. We had thought each other dead—and—Newson became her husband.'

Elizabeth broke down and wept uncontrollably. She believed this was the whole truth, and started calling Henchard her father. The father-daughter duo even went to the office of the *Casterbridge Chronicle* to change the name legally. The daughter became Elizabeth Henchard and dropped the Newson surname.

There was a shock in the offing when Henchard found the letter on Susan's deathbed. His deceased wife had written that Elizabeth was indeed Newson's daughter. Their real daughter had died three months after the drink-and-sale debacle. He was dumbstruck but he decided to make it a secret again.

Soon he started treating Elizabeth coldly and finding fault in everything she did, much to her shame and sadness. His term as a mayor was also coming to an end, which only made his life worse.

The daughter's life was as well becoming difficult but she tried to gain Henchard's favour and find time to visit her mother's grave. One day, she came across a lady reading the gravestone and chatted with her. She lived at the posh High-Place Hall and invited Elizabeth to live with her.

On an appointed day, the ladies met at the churchyard as planned. The stranger introduced herself as Miss Templeman.

A couple of days ago, Henchard had consented—and even agreed to give her an allowance—when Elizabeth told him that she wanted to move away. He was stunned when his stepdaughter told him that she was moving in to High-Place Hall. Only the previous night, Henchard had received a letter from Lucetta Templeman telling where she was in Casterbridge and asking him to visit her.

Henchard was delaying it but Lucetta

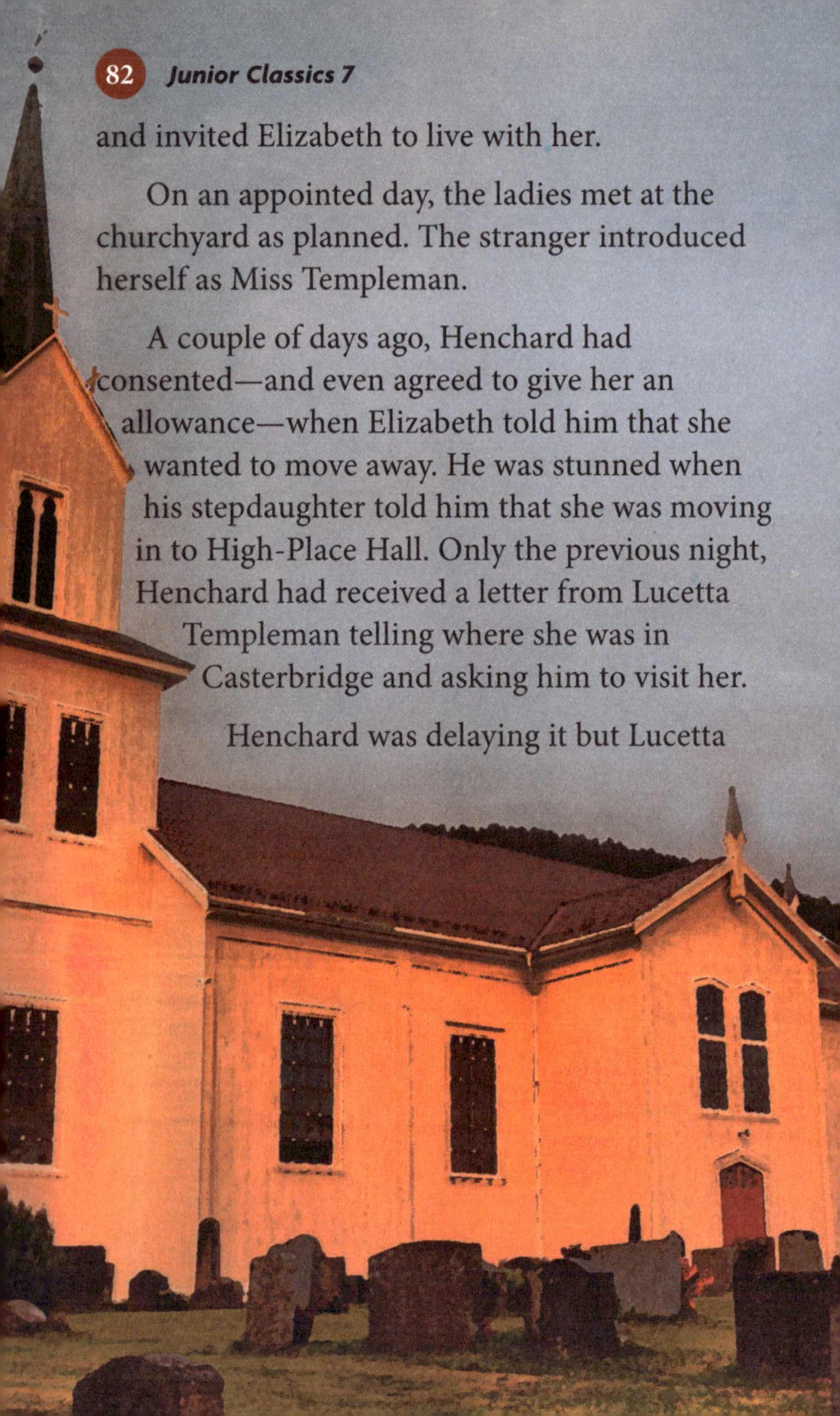

had a visitor after a few days of desperate waiting. It was Farfrae.

'I came and I inquired for Miss Henchard, and they showed me up here,' he spoke.

'You must come and sit down now,' Lucetta invited him in, 'Miss Henchard will be here soon.'

From a window, they saw the bustling marketplace. They caught the sight of a transaction, in which a young man was to leave for a distant farmland. Farfrae left, without meeting Elizabeth, and volunteered to give the man a job. Lucetta was impressed.

When the mayor arrived that day, Lucetta told the maid that she was suffering from headache and could not meet anyone. She had come to Casterbridge with a purpose and she was doing it well.

It was a Saturday morning and people were gathering at the market square. Someone had brought an exceptionally innovative seeding machine. While Farfrae appreciated the machine, Henchard demeaned it and left the place, but not before complaining to Lucetta, 'You refused to see me.'

Elizabeth heard her stepfather's word but she could not understand it. Soon, she started knowing more about Lucetta. She found that her older partner was familiar with both Farfrae and her stepfather. She was shattered that the two most important men in her life were simply indifferent towards her.

When she was out one day, Henchard came to meet Lucetta, asking for a marriage proposal.

She replied, 'For the present let things be as they are. Treat me as a friend, and I'll treat you as one. Time will—', she stopped halfway, showing like Henchard, she was haunted by the past.

He spoke again, 'You came to live in Casterbridge entirely on my account; and now you won't have anything to say to my offer!'

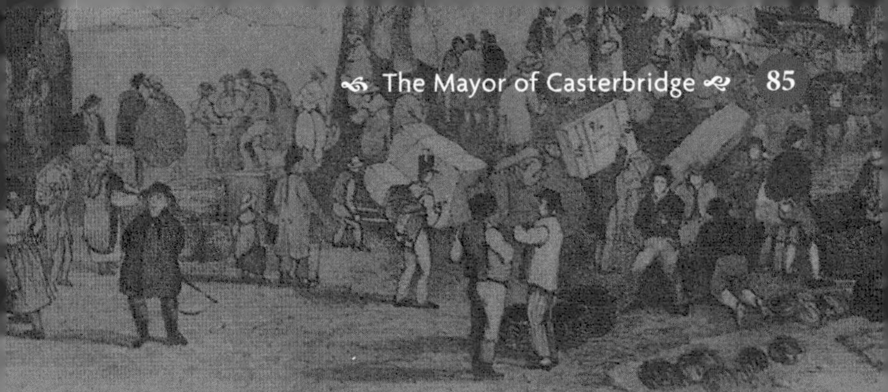

'I won't be a slave to the past—I'll love where I choose!' Lucetta said.

That was the final decision.

One spring morning, Donald Farfrae ran into his former employer, who asked him about the memory of the second woman, whom he had to break up with. When he replied positively, Henchard informed him that the woman had turned down his marriage proposal recently.

Farfrae did not figure it was Lucetta, who the mayor was talking about; and neither did Henchard know that it was because of Farfrae that Miss Templeman had snubbed his proposal. But the inevitable happened later in the day.

At the High-Place Hall, Henchard was drinking tea with Lucetta when Farfrae entered. The suspicion became obvious but nobody spoke.

In a few days, Henchard hired Joshua Jopp as a foreman, who he had ignored earlier after meeting Farfrae. He spoke aloud, 'The Scotsman, who's taking the town trade so bold into his hands, must be cut out. We'll undersell him, over-buy him and snuff him out.'

The desperation was so high that the mayor of Casterbridge even consulted a local weather forecaster, who depended on 'divine power' to predict the weather.

Unfortunately, against the diviner's prophecy of too much rainfall, the town enjoyed a normal rainy season. Apparently, Henchard lost a lot of money—he had bought too much corn for the assumed dry spell that he could not even afford!

He blamed Jopp for the misfortune and bad advice, and fired him from the job. The bad luck did not seem to end.

Before the harvest season, Farfrae was buying the grains at a low price. He had begun well and though the climate was abnormal this time, he prospered while Henchard got the second blow in as many seasons.

His business was in shambles and all he cared was to stalk Lucetta. One evening he followed her, while she was walking with Farfrae—and when she came back to her place alone, he blackmailed her to marry him.

Henchard and Lucetta did share a close romantic relationship in Jersey once, a long time ago. The breakup—if anybody knew—could have been a disgrace, especially for a lady in a conservative society. And thus Lucetta gave into the mayor's pressure.

The next day, Henchard went to the Town Hall as a magistrate, a post he had to hold for one year after the mayoral term. He reached there to find a case regarding the disorderly conduct of an old deranged woman.

When she was summoned, she started narrating, 'Twenty years ago I was selling furmity in a tent at the Weydon-Priors Fair.'

'Twenty years ago—well, suppose you go back to the beginning of the universe!' said a clerk and the people laughed aloud.

The woman continued, 'A man and a woman with a little child came into my tent where I sell furmity seasoned with rum. After drinking, he quarrelled with his wife and offered to sell her to the highest bidder. A sailor came in and bid five guineas, paid the money and led her away. The man who sold his wife in that fashion is the man sitting there in the big chair.'

She was pointing her finger at the magistrate. Everybody looked at Henchard but nobody believed her. They started expressing their disapproval, then suddenly Henchard admitted it was true and left the place. The people around the town hall stood agape.

Soon Lucetta learnt about the revelation and went to Port-Bredy, a seaside town for a few days. Casterbridge was becoming too gloomy for her. Upon returning, she found Henchard had changed his mind about marriage. Still, he needed a favour from her.

He told her, 'There is one thing you might do, Lucetta.'

It was not exactly money. He wanted her to tell Mr Grower, to whom he owed a huge debt, that they were going to marry. Perhaps that would make his creditor hopeful of getting back his money.

'I cannot!' she said.

'But why?'

'Because—he was a witness!'

Before long it dawned that Lucetta was married to Farfrae the previous week at Port-

Bredy; and Mr Grower was the witness to their low-profile marriage.

Casterbridge had never been so gloomy. The only thing left to do was to inform Elizabeth.

'You remember the story I told you of some time ago—about the first lover and the second lover?' Lucetta told Elizabeth.

'Oh yes—I remember,' replied the young lady whose world was crumbling down just like her stepfather's.

Then Lucetta narrated the whole story, as well as about the marriage. However, she said that Elizabeth was free to still stay in the same place, despite Farfrae moving in. The latter answered she would think about it. But later in the evening, she finished packing her belongings.

The world was falling apart for Michael Henchard swiftly. He lost his business. He lost his family. He lost his love. He lost everything. All that was left was his frail body and a frustrated mind. And the only asset he got was a gold watch that he was going to sell off soon. Henchard was starting to re-live his history of poverty. Such a tragic downfall of a man of character!

His stepdaughter tried several times to contact him but in vain. On the other hand, Farfrae had bought everything from him, including his office, employees and even the furniture.

The most likely future mayor, Donald Farfrae and his wife Lucetta had moved in to the house where the former mayor used to live. And Henchard was living in a shared accommodation with Jopp.

However, Farfrae was not a bad man. He did invite his ex-boss to live in the spare room but pride prompted Henchard to decline the offer. Farfrae even proposed returning the furniture but Henchard said no again.

To show his gratitude to the man who had helped in changing his life for good, Farfrae decided to buy a seed shop. He wanted to make Henchard the manager of this future store. However, he started hearing about the former mayor's hatred and planned revenge. Elizabeth had also insisted that he be cautious in dealing with her stepfather.

So, Farfrae put off his plan to buy the seed shop. Henchard was even more furious after hearing about the change of mind.

Meanwhile Lucetta was worried about the secret she shared with Henchard. Then her husband was requested by the town's council members to become the new mayor as the mayor who succeeded Henchard had died recently. Everything was happening so fast.

One morning, Henchard remembered about the letters he got from Lucetta some years back. It was in his former house. He went there without any delay.

He told Farfrae, 'I want to ask you about a packet of letters that I may possibly have left in my old safe in the dining room.'

'It must be there,' said Farfrae. 'I have never opened it at all as yet.'

'These letters are related to that unhappy business. Thank God, it is all over now.'

The former mayor explained about the letters without revealing the identity of the woman. He was reading out some of them as well.

'What has become of the poor woman?'

'Luckily she married, and married well.'

Until now, Farfrae never knew that it was his wife to whom he had once written a letter on behalf of Henchard.

It was a nightmare for Lucetta who overheard the conversation between the two men. The next day, the first thing she did was to call and meet Henchard. She asked him to destroy the letter and luckily, the man consented.

When she returned home, she met Jopp who asked her to recommend him for a job at her husband's office. He told her he came from Jersey. However, she refused and the man went back angrily.

Later, Henchard asked Jopp to deliver the packet of letters to Mrs Farfrae. On the way to delivery, Jopp halted for a few pegs of drinks at an inn, where he started reading aloud some of the letters. Then, half of the town knew the owner of the letters.

Lucetta burnt the letters as soon as she got the packet. She felt a burden off her shoulder.

Some time ago, however, the peasants had laid a good foundation for a 'skimmity-ride' after Jopp's recitation of the letters. A skimmity-ride was a spectacle to ridicule those people who were suspected of extra-marital affairs.

So, in order to save the face of their employer, some workers had already tricked Farfrae to come to a neighbouring town. A couple of hours after her husband left, Lucetta saw a commotion in the market. Elizabeth also arrived to meet her. Before the young lady could hide it, Lucetta saw the crowd. There were two effigies sitting back to back on a donkey. The figures were clearly meant for her and Henchard.

Lucetta became hysterical and collapsed on the floor. The doctor found that her condition was critical as she was pregnant too. Word was sent to fetch Farfrae. In the night, her condition slightly improved and she confessed everything to Farfrae.

When Henchard went home, Jopp told him that a man was asking for him. The younger man gave a description, 'A kind of traveller, or sea captain of some sort.' But it quickly slipped his mind.

The next morning began with a tragic news. Lucetta was dead. Elizabeth informed her stepfather, 'Mrs Farfrae! She is—dead! Yes—about an hour ago!'

After Elizabeth went, the ex-mayor was preparing for breakfast when a stranger came to meet him.

'Good morning,' greeted the stranger. 'Is it Mr Henchard I am talking to?'

'Yes, it's me.'

'Can I have a few words with you?'

'By all means.'

'You may remember me? Well—perhaps you may not. My name is Newson.'

It was the sailor, who bought his wife and baby! Henchard was speechless.

Newson narrated how circumstances compelled him to fake his death. Through

friends, Susan had learnt that their marriage, just from the sale in a drunken rage, was nonbinding. She had changed her mind, and that made him guilty. Therefore, he decided not to return home, believing Susan would go wherever she desired. He knew Susan was no more but he wanted to meet Elizabeth.

Henchard told him that the daughter was also dead. The sailor left dejected.

The former mayor had been depressed for a few days. He had even contemplated taking his own life, when he saw a figure by the pool. It was his effigy from the skimmity-ride! His own body in such a lifeless form frightened him so much. It had ironically given him a chance to be alive.

That moment of realization had also given him a chance to make amends and get closer to his stepdaughter.

Farfrae and Henchard avoided each other. Still the new mayor offered his former employer a shop.

Though Henchard had decided to give more freedom to his stepdaughter, he was

worried about losing her. He tried not to interfere between the growing intimacy between Elizabeth and Farfrae. One day, when he was snooping on her daughter and Farfrae, he saw Newson was still in town.

In the evening, Henchard informed her that he was leaving Casterbridge.

'Leave Casterbridge! Leave—me?'

Elizabeth thought it was because of Donald Farfrae.

'I don't forbid you to marry him,' said Henchard. 'Promise not to forget me when—'

He meant when Newson should come but did not mention it.

The next day when Henchard was leaving, Elizabeth followed him to the edge of the town. She hoped he might change his mind though in vain. In the evening, she accidentally met Newson at Farfrae's house.

She was excited to found her real father after such a long time. Then she discovered how Henchard had been cheating all of them. She also understood why he had left all of a sudden.

However, the good news was that they started planning for her wedding to Donald Farfrae.

Meanwhile Henchard had reached Weydon-Priors, where twenty-five years ago, a mindless auction changed his destiny. He had started working as a hay-trusser when he heard from passers-by that the wedding of Elizabeth and Farfrae was scheduled on St Martin's Day.

He arrived in Casterbridge for the wedding but there, Elizabeth treated him coldly. He departed from the house by the back door as he had arrived.

One day, a month after the wedding, Elizabeth found a cage with a dead bird inside. When she asked the maid, she was told that Henchard had brought it. She knew it was a wedding gift and a token of repentance; and it saddened her. With her husband, she started searching for her stepfather.

After a search, they traced him to one of Henchard's former employee, Abel Whittle's cottage. However, the couple were half an hour late. Henchard had passed away before they reached there.

Then Abel Whittle showed them a scrap of paper in which Henchard had written. The dead man had mentioned that nobody should tell Elizabeth of his death and that he wanted no funeral nor flower nor remembrance.

The War of the Worlds

H. G. WELLS

Part One
The Coming of the Martians

Would anyone believe that aliens, who are more intelligent than human beings, are watching us closely? It was the last part of the nineteenth century. As always, we were busy with our daily lives. It was confirmed the aliens from the planet Mars were scrutinizing and studying us, just as we would examine microbes with a microscope.

Mars revolves around the sun at a mean distance of 140,000,000 miles. It receives only half of the heat and light we get on Earth. This red planet is hardly one-seventh of the volume of our planet. It has air and water, and all that is necessary for the support of animated existence. However, we are so consumed with our pride that we cannot imagine intelligent life beyond the familiar world.

We did not know anything about the Martians. Yet it is certain how men have been so cruel and brutal. For instance in less than fifty years, the European immigrants entirely swept out the Tasmanians. Should we complain if the Martians invaded with such atrocity?

Once an astronomer, Ogilvy, invited me to the observatory at Ottershaw and we watched the strange lights and flames we had been seeing on the red planet over the last few days.

'The chances against anything man-like on Mars are a million to one,' he told me.

When I went back home, my wife was waiting for me. She pointed her finger towards the sky, and we saw the red, green and yellow signal lights hanging in a framework against the sky. The view seemed so safe and tranquil.

Later on a Thursday evening, we saw a falling star. The next morning, Ogilvy was the first to discover it. He had even contacted his friend, Henderson, a journalist who worked in London.

'Henderson,' he called, 'you saw that shooting star last night?'

'Well?' said Henderson.

'It's out on Horsell Common now.'

'Good Lord!' said Henderson. 'Fallen meteorite! That's good.'

'But it's something more than a meteorite. It's a cylinder—an artificial cylinder, man! And there's something inside.'

With a diameter of about thirty yards, the Thing was in a crater and looked a little odd, because it was cylindrical and making noises! Ogilvy had tried to open a protruding lid but it was too hot.

Henderson was interested because he had assumed that it would make a perfect news story. As expected, he went to the railway station and telegraphed the story. When I heard the story, I headed to Horsell Common in Woking.

I saw a few people had gathered there. Four to five boys were sitting on the edge of the pit. A couple of cyclists, a gardener I employed sometimes, a girl carrying a baby, Gregg the butcher and his little boy, two or three loafers and some golf caddies were curiously looking at the object. The fact was that only a very few people in England had astronomical knowledge in those days.

Later, the evening newspapers had startled London with eye-grabbing headlines. A couple of them read as:

'A MESSAGE RECEIVED FROM MARS'

'REMARKABLE STORY FROM WOKING'

More people had arrived at the scene when I went back there in the afternoon. When I went closer, I saw half a dozen men—Henderson, Ogilvy, and a tall, fair-haired man that I afterwards learned was Stent, the Astronomer Royal, with several workmen

wielding spades and pickaxes. Some of them were standing on the cylinder, which had apparently cooled off.

The next morning, more people had gathered at the site. Roughly, two or three hundred people were elbowing and jostling each other.

From the crowd, Ogilvy shouted, 'I say help keep these idiots back! We don't know what's in the strange object!'

Unexpectedly the end of the cylinder was being screwed out from within. Nearly two feet of shining screw projected. I think all of us had anticipated to see a man emerge—possibly something a little unlike us terrestrial men, but essentially a man.

However, what it occurred was beyond anyone's imagination. We saw two luminous disks that resemble eyes, something that appeared like a little grey snake, about the thickness of a walking stick, which was wriggling in the air. Gradually, a big greyish-rounded bulk, the size, perhaps, of a bear, emerged out of the cylinder. As it came out, it glistened like wet leather.

I saw one of them had two big and dark eyes that were looking at me directly. It had a V-shaped mouth without lips, under the eyes, which waggled and drop saliva. Its whole body quivered as if it was having a fit. One of its tentacles clutched the edge of the cylinder while another was swinging in the air.

Nobody had seen a Martian before. Its uneasiness, perhaps due to the greater gravitational force of the earth, was visible. Despite these, I was overcome with disgust and dread. Evidently, the gathering crowd had dispersed and many of them, including me, took cover and watched the frightening spectacle.

A strange combination of fear and curiosity engulfed me. I managed to go closer to the pit but the setting sun made it difficult to see the objects. A few more people, it seemed, shared the same feeling—and some of them went further to the edge. I joined them.

Instantly we saw, from the direction of Horsell, a group of men marching forward and the foremost of them was waving a white flag. Seemingly, as the Martians appeared to be intelligent, the marchers had presumed that they would approach with signals, showing them they were intelligent too. I learnt that Ogilvy, Stent and Henderson were in the group.

Out of the blue there was a flash of light and a quantity of luminous greenish smoke came out of the pit in three distinct puffs. It was as if some invisible jet had advanced and flashed white flames. It was as if the men with the flags were turned to fire in an instant. All I felt was that it was something very strange.

The Martians were spewing deadly heat-rays. It was terrifying because of not only the aliens, but also the silence and stillness around me in those evening hours. I realised I was in the dark common, helpless, unprotected and alone. It was too shocking. Without much thinking, I dashed towards the direction of my home.

I was exhausted with the violence of my emotion. When I reached closer home, my neighbours were still unaware about the Martians.

'People seem fair silly about the common,' said a woman over the gate. 'What's it all about?'

'Haven't you heard of the men from Mars?' said I, 'the creatures from Mars?'

'Quite enough,' she said nonchalantly.

I found my wife when I reached home. She was quite anxious when I told her about the incident. I did comfort her and myself by repeating all that Ogilvy had told me of the impossibility of the Martians establishing themselves on the earth. The most difficult thing for the aliens will be the earth's gravitational force.

The next day, people had heard of the cylinder but they were least concerned about it. In London, even Henderson's report on the Martians as well as the news about his death failed to catch anyone's attention. And in Woking, there were regular train services and passengers as always.

As contingency plan, a company of soldiers did arrive in Horsell, and they formed a cordon along the edge of the common. A second company marched through Chobham on the northern side of the common. Only the military authorities seemed to take the issue seriously.

Around midnight in Woking, people saw another cylinder falling into the pinewoods to the northwest. It had a greenish colour, and caused a silent brightness like summer lightning.

The next morning on Saturday, everyone seemed to have a shared opinion. The milkman said the military had put the condition under control. One of my neighbours echoed the same thought. A group of soldiers, whom I met near the common, told me the same thing.

I must admit that the sight of all this

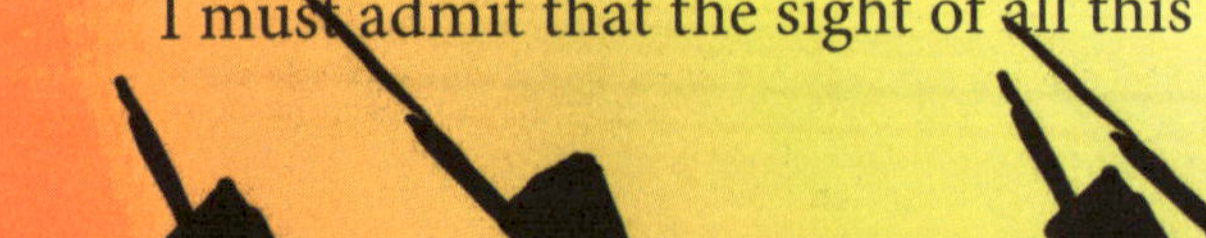

armament, all this preparation, greatly excited me. In fact, my imagination became aggressive and I thought about a dozen ways of attacking and defeating the Martians. In any way, they were lying helpless in the pit.

However, we started hearing sporadic gunshots around three o'clock. By six o'clock, there was a muffled detonation after a gust of firing. Soon, quite close to us, a violent rattling crash shook the ground. The tops of the trees burst into smoky red flame. The tower of a little church beside it sunk into ruin. The pinnacle of the mosque had vanished, and the roofline of the Oriental College itself looked as if a hundred-ton gun had been at work upon it. One of our chimneys also cracked as if a shot had hit it.

For a while, my wife and I stood motionless and awestruck. Impulsively, I hold her arm and we dashed towards the road. As my earlier thoughts of heroism against the Martians melted in a moment, I rushed inside my house and took some of our possessions.

I moved fast outside. I told my wife, 'We can't possibly stay here.'

'But where are we to go?'

She was visibly terrified.

I was clueless but I remembered her cousins at Leatherhead.

'Leatherhead!' I shouted amidst the noise.

I realized the landlord of the Spotted Dog inn had a horse and a dog cart. When I went hurriedly to meet him, he was inside the inn, more concerned about selling his pig than the events taking place outside. He consented when I told him that I'd return his horse cart by midnight. Immediately, we headed for Leatherhead.

On the way, we saw a soldier going from house to house, informing the people to evacuate.

I shouted after him, 'Any news?'

He turned, stared and yelled something about 'crawling out in a thing like a dish cover.'

We reached Leatherhead around nine o'clock. We had supper with her cousins and their families.

I had promised the innkeeper about his cart, so two hours later, I decided to head back home. Had it not been for my promise, I guessed my wife would have urged me to stay in Leatherhead that night. While I was leaving, her face was very white and pale. Soon, I headed for home taking cover in the darkness.

I reached home and fetched myself a glass of whiskey while I changed my clothes. From the window, I could see some of the destruction in the locality. Around Byfleet Courses, the heat rays had incinerated the trees, a train destroyed and some of the torched houses. It was around this time a soldier walked up to my garden.

'Hist!' said I, in a whisper.

He stood there for a while, hesitating and unsure. However, he did come closer.

'Who's there?' he said, also whispering.

'Where are you going?' I asked.

'God knows.'

'Are you trying to hide?'

'That's it.'

'Come into the house,' I offered.

I found he was an artillery driver—he had arrived at the scene around seven in the evening. It was also around the same time the Martians unleashed their deadly force. It blew up his ammunition and knocked him down on the ground. While we chatted for some time, the daybreak was approaching. And by that time, three Martian machines were visible in the pit. Never before in the history of warfare had destruction been so indiscriminate and universal.

By morning, we had separate plan. I had to go back to my wife in Leatherhead. The artilleryman had to go to his military unit in London.

As we moved out cautiously, we came across three cavalry soldiers: a lieutenant and a couple of privates of the 8th Hussars. They were unsure about the previous night's incident, so we told them the best we could. The lieutenant suggested the artilleryman should go to Weybridge, where the brigadier-general was. Thus, we lost no further time and set out for our journey.

In Weybridge, the place was comparatively peaceful; still the army men were evacuating the people. The condition was fine and we even helped some of the old people in packing up their belongings. There was another reason for the calmness. People believed that the Martians were simply formidable human beings, who might attack and sack the town and yet to be certainly destroyed in the end.

Out of nowhere, we heard some random gunshots. Until then the Martians were out of sight but it was only a matter of time. Five Martian machines approached us and I could see a heat-ray machine in the hand of one of the Martians.

Immediately, I jumped into the Thames. The water was almost boiling after one of the machines fell into the river after being hit by artillery. In an instant Weybridge turned into a complete mess. The heat ray was in its peak again. When I reached the riverbank, I saw the Martians taking away the wreckage.

Instead of going towards London, the Martians moved back to their original position in Horsell Common. Humanity was gathering for the battle while I made my way with excruciating pains and labour. Reason was the first casualty. It was a curious thing that I felt angry with my wife; I cannot account for it, but my impotent desire to reach Leatherhead worried me excessively.

I met a pastor then. He was visibly disturbed with the development in the last couple of days. I could make it out from his words.

'What does it mean?' he almost told himself. 'What do these things mean?'

I could but only stare at him and made no answer. He spoke in almost a complaining tone.

He said, 'Why are these things permitted? What sins have we done? The morning service was over. I was walking through the roads to clear my brain for the afternoon, and then—fire, earthquake, death! As if, it were Sodom and Gomorrah! All our work undone, all the work—what are these Martians?'

He had so many things to say.

'All the work—all the Sunday schools—What have we done—what has Weybridge done? Everything gone—everything destroyed. The church! We rebuilt it only three years ago. Gone! Swept out of existence! Why?'

'Things have changed,' I said, quietly. 'You must keep your head. There is still hope.'

'Hope!'

'Yes. Plentiful hope—for all this destruction!'

Then he sank into silence. In the distance, the sounds of gunshots and weird noises also subsided.

'We had better follow this path,' I suggested, 'northward to London.'

In London, things were normal as usual. My brother, who put up there as a medical student had heard nothing about the Mars attack in Woking. Even the newspapers carried reports about only the titbits.

He did learn about the news only on Saturday morning. In the dailies, however, the reports were factually incorrect. For example, in one of them, a journalist wrote that the Martians would be harmless because of the Earth's gravity. Another wrote their heat ray is a rapid firing gun.

My brother saw later in the day, and then more serious on Sunday, the hordes of people near the railway station like those in an exodus.

Soon the whole population of the great six-million city was stirring, slipping, and running.

'Black Smoke!' the voices cried. 'Fire!'

My brother began to realize the seriousness of the situation. He went hastily to his own room, put all his available money and went out into the streets.

Back in Surrey, things were as bad as ever. In fact, it was getting worse. Earlier it was only heat-ray machines, and then they got the black smoke. These were tubes that fired canisters, which upon hitting the ground, let loose black smoke and hence the name. It was heavier than air so it hung like dust above the ground. When it mixed with water, it formed a deadly powdery scum.

We heard sporadic gunshots the whole day. On that Sunday night, the fourth cylinder arrived, aggravating the condition. I learnt it fell around Bushey Park, coming down like a bright, green meteor.

Soon everybody knew the approaching doom. The brouhaha was more apparent in the mass evacuation and fleeing of people even in London. Soon the situation tuned ugly as the railway station was overcrowded. People started fighting mindlessly, while others were trampled in the commotion. Everybody was pressing and pushing for a spot inside the train.

The hysteria was incomprehensible but apparently, the trains had stopped returning to London. The engineers were afraid of both the Martians and the countless people. To put it briefly, it was the sight of a society falling apart.

My brother was near the station too. There was arson at a bicycle store and he happened to be in the mob. A cycle with a punctured tyre helped him reach Edgware quickly but it was of use no more. On the way, he saw the anxious yet helpless people. Most of them saw the mass confusion but there were little information about the real Martians and the destruction they had caused elsewhere. All of them had a similarity in their expression: that of fear.

He went there, in fact, to accompany two women there. The women were the wife and sister of a doctor, Mr George Elphinstone, who had heard about the Martians and had left to help the people. They had as well planned that the women were to stay back and inform the neighbours and the doctor was to join them the next morning, on Monday. However, it was already four hours late and he was still yet to return.

Impatience was visible on everyone's faces. My brother and the women had no choice but to scuttle through the mad crowd.

If one could have flown on a balloon in the blazing blue above London, any viewer would see the black dots of people in a complete chaos, running and rushing in every possible direction. Besides, each dot represented a human agony of terror and physical distress. On the other hand by Monday evening, the seventh Martian cylinder had fallen.

On Wednesday, finally, my brother and his company got the seat on a ship that sailed to Ostend in Belgium. Everybody was charged an exorbitant amount for the tickets, but nobody seemed to have a problem as long as they could get out from there.

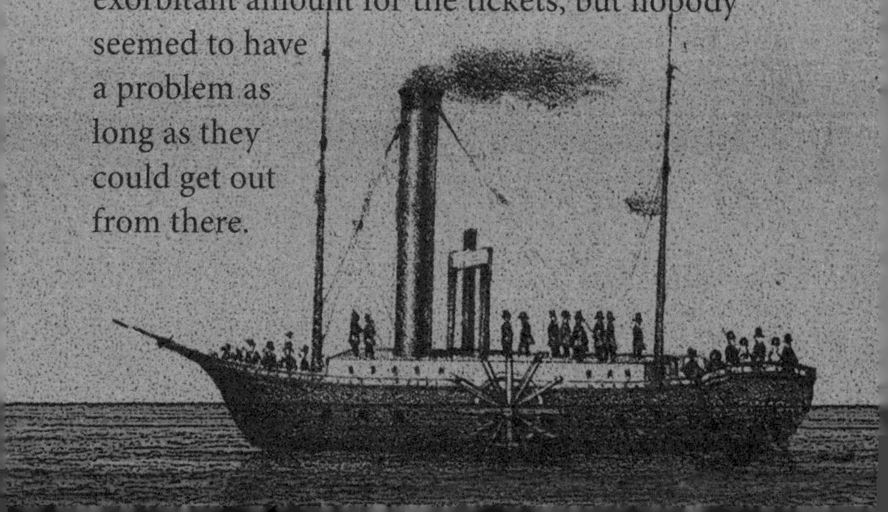

Incidentally, just as the ship was about to start its journey, passengers saw the Martian tripods. My brother was more surprised than being afraid. The aliens had started attacking but fortunately, Thunder Child, a torpedo, destroyed two of the tripods. Everybody cheered while the fear psychosis was still evident on many faces.

Soon the ship was able to continue its journey without further hiccups.

Part Two
The Earth under the Martians

On this side of the world, the pastor and I had to spend two more nights in an abandoned house. Everything was fine as long as we got rid of the black smoke. Earlier he was reluctant to leave, while I had to go to Leatherhead at any cost. The fear of solitude prompted him to join me.

During the day, we had to hide in a ditch. In front of us, what could have been extraordinary was becoming so common. For instance, the Martians were picking up the people and throwing them in a basket. Gradually, we reached Sheen and decided to take a break. We broke into another deserted house.

Before we realized there was a loud crash. I had almost lost consciousness when the pastor whispered that I should not make any noise. Some Martians were seemingly outside the house.

At daybreak, we saw a tripod through a hole in the wall. I learnt it was one of the cylinders; and it had landed just in front of the house. Still we didn't move an inch and were controlling the sound of our breath.

Within such a close distance, I could make out their physical structure and weapons. The Martians had handling machines—it was a sort of metallic spider with five jointed, agile legs, and with an extraordinary number of jointed levers, bars, and reaching and clutching tentacles about its body. Physically, a Martian had only brain and nerves. It had a head, nearly four feet in diameter. The two eyes looked similar to us but it was of blue and violet. It had an ear on the back of its head, yet no nose. From the view, I can see it had a lung too.

From their eyes, it looked the aliens communicate through telepathy. They did make sounds, which was more of a noise than communication. Then, it was the turn for the pastor to see the view from the peephole.

It was just the beginning. On the third day when we were trapped inside the house, patience was running out. In as many days, I saw the Martians killed a man and a boy. Right away, I started digging a tunnel, but it collapsed making a dull sound. Still, luck was still on our side. The Martians had left the pit!

When we looked back, it was sixth day we had been hiding in that house. The pastor was becoming mad as well. It sounds paradoxical, but I was inclined to think that the weakness and insanity of the pastor warned me, braced me and kept me a sane man. Otherwise, his voice was becoming louder each day and he was overeating all the time.

'It is just, O God!' he repeatedly mumbled. 'It is just. On me and mine be the punishment laid. We have sinned, we have fallen short. There was poverty, sorrow; the poor were trodden in the dust, and I held my peace. I preached acceptable folly—my God, what folly!—When I should have stood up, though I died for it, and called upon them to repent—repent! ... Oppressors of the poor and needy ...! The wine press of God!'

'Be still!' I requested.

I was more afraid than hitting him—but I stroked lightly with a meat chopper on his head to let him see some reason. He fell on the ground. Around this time, I saw one of the Martian's limbs coming slowly across the hole. I was trembling like crazy but did manage to enter into the coal cellar. Had the Martian seen me? What was it doing now? I had no answers. To my horror, the Martians had dragged out the pastor through one of their tentacles.

On the eleventh day, I decided I should go out of the cellar. I saw that I was out of food supply but I was helpless. The next day, I cannot hold any longer; and I rushed to a water pump. This action continued for more days. On the fifteenth day, I saw a dog. I thought if I could induce him to come into the place quietly I should be able, perhaps, to kill and eat him; and in any case, it would be advisable to kill him, lest his actions attracted the attention of the Martians. Yet the dog left before I can make any decision.

I heard no sound anymore on the fifteenth day, so I risked and looked outside. There were no sign of the Martians. I went outside and it was such a great feeling. The sky was too bright and the air was so sweet. These things had become a luxury for me. Meanwhile, Sheen was deserted and the place was covered with weeds.

It was better to get moving when I had the chance. I moved towards the west, away from London. The condition made me think that I was the sole survivor. Lucky for me, but it was spine chilling to think about the Martians creating havoc in other places. Within such a short period, the world seemed to have changed beyond any reason and imagination.

When it was dark, I broke into an inn this time. After such a long time, I felt somehow normal. Still the thoughts of my wife and the pastor bogged me down. Simultaneously, I was gathering courage from the rats and frogs that had survived independent of the Mars attack.

The next day I met a man so unexpectedly.

'It is you,' he was also surprised, 'the man from Woking. And you weren't killed at Weybridge?'

I recognized him at the same moment.

'You are the artilleryman who came into my garden.'

'Good luck!' he said.

'Have you seen any Martians?" I asked.

'They've gone away across London,' he was aware. 'I guess they've got a bigger camp there. Of a night, all over there, Hampstead way, the sky is alive with their lights.'

'It is all over with humanity,' I hardly saw any hope. 'If they can do that they will simply go round the world.'

However, I saw as well that he had a brilliant idea. He wanted to form a group of strong people who would live in London's underground drains. They would leave the Martians to mind their own business while they gathered enough scientific solutions to dispose of the Martians. Then he took me to a ditch where he had been working on.

An hour later, I left him with his grand plan but I'd admit there was little hope in his dreams. It was too hopelessly idealistic in those bleak days; neither it was practical at all.

London was completely in mess. The only certain thing seemed to be the recurring violence. The view never got better: deserted streets, burning houses, pervasive mess and what not. The farther I went into the city, the deeper grew the stillness. Surprisingly it was not so much the stillness of death rather it was the stillness of suspense, of expectation.

The next day it was no different. The time was just past twelve noon. I wondered if I was the only man alive in this city of dead. I wondered about my friends whom I had forgotten for years. I started feeling extremely lonely.

Then an insane thought struck me. I would die and end it. I was even about to save myself from the trouble of killing myself and headed towards the direction of a Martian cylinder towards Primrose Hill. And I saw the most unexpected thing! The Martians were dead!

Around the crater, there were huge mounds of materials and strange shelter places. Everything was lying scattered as well—some of the dead Martians in their overturned war machines, some of them holding their machines. Stark and silent, the Martians were lying dead.

The cause of death: putrefactive and disease bacteria against which the Martians' systems were unprepared. I stood staring into the pit, and my heart lightened gloriously.

Finally, the destruction was over; and probably the healing would begin soon. The survivors, then scattered across the country—despite being leaderless, lawless, foodless, like sheep without a shepherd—would as well return before long. Along with the newfound excitement, I felt an overwhelming force, thinking about myself, my wife, and about the old life of hope and tender helpfulness.

Later, I found that I was not the first person to learn about the Martians' death. Several people had seen it the previous night. Indeed, one of the men had sent the news report to Paris already. I met them only after I had yelled insanely, 'The Last Man Left Alive! Hurrah! The Last Man Left Alive!'

Some of the strangers told me, after hearing about my story that Leatherhead had been completely wiped out. For four days, I took refuge with a family. I was feeling so lonely and dejected again. All I wanted was to see what had remained of the little life that seemed so happy and bright in my past. Yet, everything seemed to be in vain.

I could not resist anymore. So, I promised the family that I would return and went out again into the streets that had lately been so dark and strange and empty. I could see from the people and their activities that life was returning to normal, albeit slowly. I knew my destination and headed to the railway station.

I reached my house before I knew it. I went in unhurriedly though it was the first time I was going back there in four weeks. In my study room, the curtains were fluttering and nobody had closed it ever since I left it with the artilleryman. Then I went into the dining room. The room showed the sign of neglect and lack of maintenance. It was around this time I had a surprise. I heard a voice from the back:

'It is no use. The house is deserted. No one has been here these ten days. Do not stay here to torment yourself. No one escaped but you.'

When I turned back, I could hardly believe my eyes. I was both amazed and afraid. There they were my wife and my cousin.

'I'm back,' she gave a faint cry. 'I knew—knew...' Before she could continue I went up to her and hold her tight in my arms.

It had been the strangest things in the history of humanity. We might never know about the heat ray and the black smoke. However, for certain, human beings are not alone in this universe.

Amongst these developments, there was one more thing that was the strangest of all. I got the chance to hold my wife's hand again—while I had counted her, and that she had counted me, among the dead.

Other Titles *In the* Series

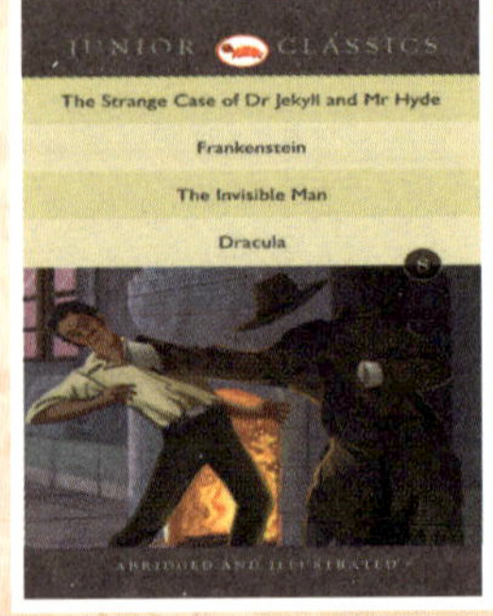